"Scared to death . . . scared to death. . . . Little Bobby's scared to death. . . ."

Bobby Wimmer would never forget what the Five did to him. The Five: Ben, Carlyn, Brooke, Jamie, and Leigh. They dared him to go into the old Whitlock Mansion, and when he didn't make it out, they left him there to die. . . .

He'll never forget the darkness, the smell, the rats, the screaming. . . .

Now it's six years later. Bobby's ready for revenge. He's going to scare them so bad, they'll want to die. He's going to scare them to death.

Bobby killed Leigh. Who will be his next victim . . . ?

**The SCARED TO DEATH trilogy, by Ted Pickford:**

**BOBBY'S WATCHING
BOBBY'S BACK
BRIDESMAIDS IN BLACK**

# SCARED TO DEATH

## Bobby's Back

TED PICKFORD

**BANTAM BOOKS**

TORONTO · NEW YORK · LONDON · SYDNEY · AUCKLAND

SCARED TO DEATH: BOBBY'S BACK
A BANTAM BOOK 0 553 40778 3

First published in USA by Bantam Books

First publication in Great Britain

Published by arrangement with Bantam Doubleday Dell Books for
Young Readers, a division of Bantam Doubleday Dell Publishing
Group, Inc.

PRINTING HISTORY
Bantam edition published 1994

Bantam Books are published by Transworld Publishers Ltd,
61–63 Uxbridge Road, Ealing, London W5 5SA,
in Australia by Transworld Publishers (Australia) Pty Ltd,
15–25 Helles Avenue, Moorebank, NSW 2170,
and in New Zealand by Transworld Publishers (NZ) Ltd,
3 William Pickering Drive, Albany, Auckland.

Printed and bound in Great Britain by
Cox & Wyman Ltd, Reading, Berkshire

# BOBBY'S BACK

# CHAPTER 1

Bobby Wimmer smiled as he jabbed the thumbtack into the girl's head.

Hey—it was only a photograph. The tack wouldn't hurt her. In fact, nothing would hurt her now. Because pretty little Leigh Millen was dead.

Bobby stepped back to admire his handiwork and grinned. Victim number one. And around her, his future victims, numbers two through five.

He had pinned the snapshot to the wall of his new studio apartment. So far, this was the only wall he had decorated. Newspaper clippings, photos, and other reminders were tacked up neatly. They all had one thing in common. They were all about the Five.

An article from the Middletown paper announced Carlyn Alexander's Westinghouse scholarship to Indiana Tech; another from the school paper celebrated Brooke Tremont's victory at the cheerleading competitions; another story touted Ben Douglas as an all-state high school baseball star. And then there were photographs—pictures of the twins, Jamie and Leigh Millen, and of the others—each photo a candid shot, each subject totally unaware of the photographer.

The Five. They were five normal-looking teenagers unaware that they had ruined Bobby Wimmer's life when he was twelve. One had paid the price with her life, and four were about to.

As Bobby studied Leigh's smile his own grin broadened.

Poor little Leigh. She'd looked so peaceful after she died, lying at the bottom of that elevator shaft, a tangle of limbs and golden hair. Nothing in his life had given him the rush he'd gotten from killing Leigh. It had made all his suffering worthwhile.

As he studied the pictures on his wall, his glance fell on the other blond and blue-eyed girl, Leigh's sister Jamie. Except for Jamie's short hair and a few extra inches of height, the twins looked identical. But there was one very crucial difference. Jamie was still alive.

Bobby had gone after Jamie when he'd finished with Leigh. He'd driven from Leigh's campus in Madison, Wisconsin, to Jamie's in Northern Illinois. He'd liked the order of it; there was a certain symmetry in getting rid of the twins first. But now Jamie would have to wait. She was hot, surrounded by police ever since he'd paid her a little visit. He hadn't really hurt her—just given her a good scare. He wanted Jamie Millen to know he was after her —and that he'd be back.

It was time to change plans. His eyes went to the map of the Midwest he'd pinned beneath the photos. He'd leave Jamie alone until some of the hysteria died down. His gaze came to rest on Indiana. He'd go to Indiana Tech. It was Carlyn Alexander's turn to die.

Bobby's smile faded. There was a lot of work still to be done. Hurriedly, he tugged on a pair of tight black jeans and a black sweater.

He picked the phone up off the floor and checked the receiver one last time, getting a dial tone. The phone company had gotten the thing turned on at last. He punched in a number from memory.

"Hi, Debbie," he said when a familiar voice answered.

Bobby had met Debbie Holgate in his last foster home, where they became close friends. They'd kept in touch over the years, and now they were more than friends.

"Bobby! Where are you? I've been really worried and—"

"Debbie, listen," he said as gently as he could. "I can't talk right now, I'm in a rush. I've got some very important business and I've got to take care of it right away. But I just wanted to call you so you know I'm fine, and—"

"But, Bobby, I don't even—"

"I'll call you back and we can catch up, okay? Tonight, I promise. But I really have to run. Bye."

Feeling a mild twinge of regret, he pressed down the receiver button, cutting off her protest.

Then he checked his reflection in the cracked mirror he had rescued from the trash. The image he saw still startled him. With his dyed-red hair and the new glasses covering his deep-set brown eyes, he almost didn't recognize himself. Which was fine. Because it meant that the four remaining members of the Five wouldn't recognize him either. Not even Jamie.

He flicked the lights and went out the door.

As he started down the building's dingy steps, he began to hum.

"Scared to death . . . scared to death . . . little Carlyn's scared to death."

# CHAPTER 2

Carlyn Alexander lifted a stack of thick science textbooks, revealing a worn blue upholstered cushion beneath them. "I knew there was a chair somewhere under here," she said, smiling at her friend Jamie Millen.

Jamie was staring at a photograph pinned to the bulletin board above Carlyn's desk. It showed a line of five grubby ten-year-olds, all of them mugging for the camera. Carlyn and Brooke Tremont stood with their arms around each other's shoulders. Carlyn was sticking her tongue out at the camera, and Brooke was holding two fingers behind Ben Douglas's head. Jamie stood next to Carlyn, making a funny face. On the end of the line Leigh, Jamie's twin, was collapsing in giggles.

5

Carlyn handed Jamie a cup of hot cocoa. "We were obnoxious even then."

Jamie nodded. "Except for Leigh." She sat down on the chair, and Carlyn curled up against the pillows that covered her bed.

Carlyn waited, wondering if Jamie wanted to talk about her sister, but Jamie was silent, her eyes focused on the mug in her hand. *What can I say?* Carlyn wondered. *And how can it be so hard to talk to someone I've known since I was ten?*

"I'm glad you stopped by on your way back to school," she said at last. "Even if it is only for a few hours."

Jamie shrugged. "It was on my way."

Carlyn knew Jamie had just come from visiting her parents in Middletown. Carlyn took a breath, unsure of whether Jamie was willing to talk about what was going on at home. "How are they?" she asked. "Your parents, I mean."

Jamie ran a hand through her short blond hair. "Not great. They want me to take the rest of the semester off and go home. They think I'd be safer there."

"They might be right, after what you went through with that psycho," Carlyn said.

"I got away from him." Jamie's voice was flat. "Home is the worst place of all for me. Everything in that house reminds me of Leigh. Besides, it's been nearly six weeks since . . ."—she let the words "the attack" go unspoken—"and the police haven't come up with anything."

Carlyn frowned. "You know," she said, "I've

been thinking that whoever the murderer is, it's got to be someone you and Leigh know. Maybe it's even someone from high school." *Someone I know,* Carlyn added silently.

Jamie frowned. "I just can't imagine who would hate us enough to do something like this. Leigh never made an enemy in her life."

"I know what you're saying. But there must be someone out there who has something against you or your family."

"Well, I can't think of anybody," Jamie said grimly. "Nothing in my life ever prepared me for this. Except horror movies." She finished her cocoa and looked around the narrow dorm room at the shelves filled with Carlyn's science and lab books. "To tell you the truth, I'd really like to change the subject. Talking about this really makes me sick."

"I know, but I can't help thinking—what if he didn't get scared off last time? I think we've got to try to remember as much as we can from high school, from grammar school . . . Who would have a motive to hurt you or Leigh? How about Ben?"

"Ben Douglas?" Jamie nearly laughed. "Mr. Straight Arrow Perfect Person? No way. You should see him now. He's captain of everything and ridiculously good-looking too. Stanford is supposed to give him some big sports scholarship. I don't see why he'd want to hurt us."

"I didn't mean as a suspect," Carlyn said. "I was thinking we should talk to him and Brooke and all the other kids we used to hang out with.

Maybe someone will remember something." She hesitated, thinking about Ben. "Hey, how do you know all that stuff about Ben? Have you talked to him lately?"

"No. We haven't talked in a while. I guess his being a year younger caught up with our friendship. But my mom and his mom are still friends, since they're neighbors and everything," Jamie answered.

"Hmm . . ." Carlyn said thoughtfully. "I think you should give him a call. Since he still lives in Middletown, and practically lives across the street from your folks, he may know something we don't know."

Jamie shrugged. "I guess . . ."

"Wait a second, did you hear that sound?" Carlyn asked. She stood up slowly and turned toward the door.

Jamie listened for a moment. "I thought I heard a footstep."

Carlyn stood motionless, her ears straining to pick up every sound. The loudest was the wind moving through the trees outside the dorm, but she could also hear her own heart beating furiously. Because there *was* another sound, just outside her door. Jamie's face went pale with fear, and Carlyn felt her own body tense.

Suddenly Carlyn moved to the door. She pulled it open and stepped into the hall.

Something *was* out there. Carlyn caught a glimpse of it—and screamed.

# CHAPTER 3

Carlyn's heart pounded as she peered into the shadows.

In a second Jamie stood beside Carlyn. "What is it?"

"Someone was there," she whispered. "I *know* I saw someone."

Jamie stepped farther into the hallway and looked around. "There's no one out there," she said.

Carlyn nodded, wondering if her imagination was getting the best of her. She looked carefully around. There was no sign of anyone.

"But someone *was* there," she said. "I'd bet my life that there was a man standing here, right outside my door."

. . .

Bobby Wimmer crouched as still as he could in the broom closet of Carlyn Alexander's dorm hall, listening.

He fought down a surge of annoyance. He hadn't meant for Carlyn to hear him listening by the door. He wasn't ready to give himself away. Worse, Jamie was there, and she and Carlyn were trying to figure out his identity. That was something he hadn't counted on.

He'd deliberately left Jamie alone because her place was crawling with cops. The last thing he needed was for her to team up with Carlyn and the two of them to play detective.

He'd been counting on killing Carlyn next. Like Leigh, Carlyn would be an easy victim. And here he was, right inside her dorm. He could do it quickly—

He weighed this against his ultimate goal—killing *all* of the Five without getting caught, and making sure they all suffered the same kind of terror he'd known in the old Whitlock place. Which meant he couldn't afford to have any of them figure out his identity until it was too late, until they were moments from death.

Carlyn, trying to remember everyone they knew from Middletown, was getting close. Too close. And Jamie's appearance was not a good sign. For all he knew, Jamie had cops following her. Maybe he ought to forget the girls for a while and let them both get distracted by other things. Maybe now was the time to stalk someone who wasn't thinking about Leigh's killer at all.

He'd let Jamie and Carlyn think they were safe for a while. He'd leave them on their college campuses and let them forget how much danger they were in.

As for him, in a few weeks he'd go back to Middletown. Now, he decided, it was Ben Douglas's turn to die.

# CHAPTER 4

"Thanks for the ride," Ben Douglas said as his friend Kyle parked his Volvo across the street from the Middletown gym.

"Sure," said Kyle.

Ben reached back for his black gym bag, then started to open the door, but Kyle put a hand out to stop him. "Ben, could I say something?"

"Shoot," said Ben.

"It's Friday," Kyle began. "You just pitched another game that wasn't so . . . great."

"Thanks," Ben said sarcastically. "I really needed you to remind me of that."

"I'm *not* trying to rub it in," Kyle said. "I'm trying to tell you that you're pushing yourself too hard. Everyone deserves a break now and then. Even you."

"Maybe you're right." Ben leaned back in the seat and closed his eyes. He opened them immediately. "Okay," he said with a smile, "I took a break." He was out of the car and crossing the street before Kyle could object.

The gym's neon sign flashed: MUSCLE POWER. Ben entered the narrow outer door and went into the locker room, where he changed into sweats, a muscle shirt, and a wide weight-lifter's belt.

Inside the gym, a number of weight lifters were making their way along the circuit of Nautilus equipment.

Louis Ramirez greeted him. The short, fit trainer was working the front desk. "It's Ben 'The Machine' Douglas."

Ben knew everyone at the gym, and everyone knew him. Which was why the new guy caught his eye right away.

He was maybe nineteen, twenty tops, with red hair and glasses. He was wearing black Sander Community College sweats and a heavy-duty black weight-lifter's belt. He had ripped off the sleeves of his gray sweatshirt to show off long, powerful arms. The guy had definitely been training somewhere. His deep-set brown eyes met Ben's for a moment, then he looked away and continued his stretching.

Ben sat down on the mats and started in on his own stretching routine. He glanced at the guy a few times, but the newcomer never looked his way.

His stretches done, Ben headed for the first ma-

13

chine in the gym's Nautilus circuit—the overhead pull. He set the weight for a hundred pounds and started his repetitions, pulling the bar down again and again.

He was finishing rep number six when he sensed the new guy standing there, watching. As soon as Ben got up from the machine, the new guy reached down and changed the weight setting. Ben couldn't resist glancing back to see which setting the stranger used. He felt a surge of surprise as he realized that he'd raised the weight to one hundred and twenty.

You have enough to worry about without getting into a competition with some stranger, Ben told himself. But at every machine, the guy outlifted Ben. Almost without being conscious of what he was doing, Ben began setting his own weights higher than usual. He couldn't help it.

A few of the regulars at the gym had even stopped to watch. "Hey, Ben. You finally met your match, huh?" called Louis from behind the counter.

Ben was moving through the machine circuit faster now, breathing harder. His T-shirt was already soaked with sweat. Behind him, the stranger didn't even appear to be working hard.

"C'mon, Ben!" called a skinny old man who was pedaling an Exercycle. "You can beat this guy!"

Ben felt a familiar rush of adrenaline—the same feeling he had when he walked up to the mound to pitch. He knew that every eye was on him.

Slowly, he walked over to the Smith machine, the last stop on the Nautilus circuit.

"Looks like we saved the best for last," the red-haired guy said.

"Looks like we did," answered Ben grimly.

Ben stepped aside and gestured—after you. The stranger loaded the extra free weights onto the barbell, then looked up at the sign on the wall. "NOTE: THIS MACHINE CANNOT BE USED WITHOUT A SPOTTER. The Management."

The Smith machine was probably the only really dangerous exercise machine in the gym. The machine had a large black metal frame, like a guillotine. Resting on this frame was a huge barbell with a metal hook on each end. The weight lifter belted himself into a leather seat right under the barbell. When he finished his reps he twisted the barbell so the hooks fit over the notches in the frame, holding the barbell safely in place. But if the lifter was too tired to raise the hooks to the first notch, he was trapped under the huge weight. That was where the spotter came in. In an emergency, the spotter could replace the barbell safely on the frame.

The red-haired guy turned to Ben. "Will you spot me?"

"Sure," Ben said, careful to keep his voice neutral.

The stranger wiped off the leather seat with his towel and slipped into position.

Ben helped the guy twist the barbell so the hooks came off the notches in the frame and the

15

full two hundred forty pounds settled onto the stranger's gloved hands.

The guy grunted. Okay, Ben thought, at least I know he's human. He was lowering the weight now. Ben could see the blood pounding into his face. He's a goner, thought Ben with relief. Look at the way he's struggling. And bringing the barbell down was the easy part.

But now the guy was pushing the barbell all the way back up. First rep.

There were impressed murmurs. The guy lowered the weight again. Then back up. Again and again. Eight reps. Nine. Only one more!

The guy was struggling. His arms were buckling.

But just then the stranger pressed his gym shoes hard into the floor, bucked against the seat, and pressed the barbell all the way up. He twisted the barbell himself, hooking it onto the frame without Ben's help.

There was a smattering of applause. The stranger was gasping for breath. He got up and started toweling off the seat.

"Okay," Ben said, trying to stay calm. "So I've got to do two-fifty." He slipped the black doughnut-shaped weights onto either end of the barbell.

All eyes were on Ben now. "Ben," Louis said, "you sure you want to do this? That's about thirty pounds over—"

"Lou," Ben cut him off, "I know what I'm doing."

The red-haired stranger was watching him, his

arms crossed, his face blank. "I'll spot you," he told Ben.

Ben got into position under the barbell and fastened the belt. He felt as if he were strapping himself into an electric chair.

"Ready?" asked the stranger.

"Sure," said Ben. But he didn't feel ready at all.

The stranger shrugged and twisted the huge barbell back so the hooks came off the frame—

The barbell went down so fast there was a gasp from the crowd. Ben's eyes went wide. Every muscle in his face, neck, arms, abdomen, and chest was straining. He could feel his face turning deep red, almost blue, with effort.

I'm a dead man, he thought.

But then—somehow—the barbell started to rise. Ben summoned his last reserves of strength. Just a few more inches.

Suddenly, a bolt of pain shot through his arms. I can't make it, he thought.

His arms gave out completely, and the gigantic weight crashed down toward his chest.

A grim thought flashed like lightning through Ben's mind.

This is it. I'm going to be crushed to death.

# CHAPTER 5

T he red-haired stranger moved fast. He grabbed the barbell and twisted it so that it hooked over the very last pair of notches in the frame.

Ben felt a shudder of relief go through him. The massive barbell was now resting safely—only inches over his throat. His entire body was shaking with the strain. It felt as if every muscle in his body had dissolved.

I can't believe I just did that, he thought, amazed at his own stupidity. He'd let himself get pushed into taking on more weight than he could safely lift, and it had nearly killed him.

The red-haired stranger helped him out from under the barbell. "You okay?" he asked.

"Fine," Ben said. He didn't feel fine, though. He felt as if he were going to throw up. He looked around. He was still the center of attention. Everyone in the gym had just watched him humiliate himself.

Louis stood glaring at him, his hands on his hips. "This machine is not for games," he said angrily. "Remember that."

Louis turned and headed back to his desk as the others in the gym began to return to their own workouts.

"Well, looks like you won," Ben told the stranger.

"Won?" The other guy looked surprised. "Hey, there are no losers in a good workout, right?"

Ben felt a surprised wave of relief. He wasn't going to rub it in.

His competitor held out his hand. "Al Dalton."

"Ben Douglas." They shook hands.

"You're good," Bobby, alias Al, said. "No one in my old gym even came close to what you were doing. You ever cotrain?"

"Nope."

Bobby nodded. "You don't like someone holding you back, right? I'm the same way. But I always thought, if I could hook up with someone who was really serious about getting in top shape, you know, we could push each other harder. What do you think?"

Ben thought for a moment. "It could be great, but I really can't take on anything else right now," he said honestly. "I can't even handle the schedule I've already got."

"That's where cotraining can help," Bobby

said. "You can get more done in a shorter amount of time. And it motivates you, too."

Ben shook his head. "I don't know, man."

"Try it for two weeks," Bobby urged. "If you don't get results, we'll drop it." He grinned at Ben, his smile surprisingly infectious.

Why *not* try? Ben thought. Maybe it will change my luck. He held out his gloved hand. "Tomorrow at four."

"At four."

They slapped a hard high five, sealing the bargain.

We just sealed your fate, buddy, thought Bobby "Al Dalton" Wimmer as he watched Ben make his way toward the locker room. Ben walked slowly, as if every muscle in his body ached.

Yeah, you're hurting, Bobby thought. But look at it this way, Ben, I could have killed you just then. But that would have been too easy, wouldn't it? First, you and I are going to have some fun.

"Ben! Over here!"

A pretty brunette called to Ben as Bobby trailed him into Pepe's Pizza Parlor after their Friday night workout. "I'll go crazy if I don't do *something* that's not work," Ben had said in the locker room. "Want to come?"

Pepe's was the high school hangout, and Ben obviously ran with the coolest crowd in the school. Bobby felt a surprising touch of his old envy as other kids came up to Ben, slapping him on the back, trying to get him to sit at their tables. And Bobby lost count of the number of girls who tried to get Ben's attention, as if he were some kind of rock star.

Ben made straight for a table at the very back of the pizza parlor. There he introduced "Al" to a handsome dark-haired boy named Kyle and another boy named Scott, both of whom were on the baseball team. Sitting between them was one of the prettiest girls Bobby had ever seen. She was small and slim, with short dark hair, almond-shaped green eyes, and fine, perfect features. Her name was Megan. She had the kind of beauty models had. Bobby looked at her and for a moment he wasn't sure she was real.

"Hi," she said, holding out a hand to him. "Ben told me he'd found a partner for cotraining."

Bobby nodded, suddenly feeling as shy as he'd been as a kid.

"I shouldn't be nice to you," she went on in a teasing tone.

"Why not?" Bobby asked, immediately on guard.

Meg's green eyes were dancing with humor. "Because Ben already spends more time with the Nautilus machines than with me," she answered. "Training with you only makes it worse."

"No," Bobby said. "Cotraining is a more efficient workout." Bobby winked at her. "He'll actually spend less time in the gym."

"If that's really the truth, then I owe you one," Meg said, giving him a big smile.

Bobby smiled, wondering what it would feel like to kiss her. "I'll be sure to call in the debt."

Ben put an arm around Meg, pulling her close and dropping a kiss against her hair. "As soon as I hear about the scholarship, we'll have more time," he said. "I promise."

Kyle yawned loudly. "This is all very touching," he said, "but will you two knock it off? We're trying to order a pizza here. Dalton, how do you feel about pepperoni?"

Bobby stumbled over an answer, unable to believe that Ben's friends accepted him so easily. Back when he was twelve, all Bobby wanted was to be part of Ben's circle. To be one of the Five. Now the Five were gone but Ben was still at the center of the coolest clique in Middletown, and suddenly he was part of it too.

And now I don't need it, he reminded himself. Now I'm going to destroy its center.

But as the meal went on Bobby found himself increasingly drawn into the conversation. He, Ben, Scott, and Kyle talked baseball, stereo systems, cars, and even workouts.

"Time out," Meg called at one point, setting down her slice of pizza. "We've got to talk about something I'm interested in too. You've got a choice: dating in the nineties or the rise in serial killers in American society."

Bobby stiffened. Why did she have to say that? He'd been feeling so comfortable with these people, like he was really a part of things.

"Oh, please," Kyle groaned.

Ben grinned. "On behalf of those of us with weaker stomachs, I'd like to request another change of subject."

"Girls," Scott said quickly.

Meg winked at Bobby. "We'll just have to go off on our own and have a real conversation without these dweebs."

"Obviously," Bobby agreed quickly.

"So, Al," Meg said. "What do *you* think about dating in the nineties?"

"Watch how you answer that," Ben warned, draping a possessive arm around Meg's shoulders. "I'm the only guy Meg will be dating in the nineties—or any other decade."

Better enjoy yourself, Bobby thought. The nineties are almost over for you, bud.

Meg sighed and kissed Ben on the cheek. "You're a little too sure of yourself, but I'm crazy about you anyway."

"Thanks a lot." Ben tugged gently on her hair, then stood up. "It's been real," he said to the others, "but I've got to go. I've got practice early tomorrow with my dad."

He reached out a hand for Megan, who stood up and leaned comfortably against him. "Later," she said, smiling at Bobby. With Ben's arm around her they walked out, the perfect high school couple.

Later that night Bobby lay awake, staring at the ceiling. This was a new experience for him. He was *never* an insomniac. He turned over restlessly.

At four in the morning he finally gave up on sleep and got out of bed. As usual when he got up, he automatically went to the wall where he'd put up the pictures of the Five. Now his eyes focused on Ben. As a kid Ben had been a bully with a mean streak that would have been considered impressive even in reform school.

Now he was different. Seven years later his mean streak had mellowed into a competitive edge. He was a handsome, self-confident athlete, not a bully. He had the games, the grades, the girl. And he was finally ready to be Bobby's friend.

And then he realized what had kept him awake. The evening he'd just spent with Ben and his friends had been one of the best times of his life.

"Too late now, Douglas," Bobby said aloud. "You've got everything—but I'm going to take it all away from you, one by one. I'll take away your girlfriend, I'll ruin your grades, I'll flush your scholarship down the drain. And when you've got nothing left—when all you are is a whining little wimp—that's when I'll finally show some mercy.

"That's when I'll kill you."

# CHAPTER 6

Ben jerked open his gym locker, pulled his T-shirt off, and tossed it onto the floor. It had been another lousy baseball practice. He'd pitched nothing but balls all afternoon, and his arm was killing him.

He opened a jar of muscle liniment, rubbing it into his sore arm as his teammates filed in. The ointment burned pleasantly, warming his muscles.

Kyle pulled his locker open, then let out a yelp. "Hey!"

The other guys gathered around to look, laughing. Ben peered into the locker. It looked as if someone had puked all over Kyle's shoes.

Chip Jacobson reached in and picked up the slimy mess, holding it up for everyone to see. Plastic joke vomit.

"I knew it all along," said Kyle, obviously relieved. "Is it yours, Jacobson?"

"Not this time," said Chip. "I think somebody's trying to get you back for leaving Jell-O in his cap."

"Or could it be the Krazy Glue you mixed with the batter's rosin?" another guy put in.

Kyle turned to the third baseman. "Jon?"

Jon shook his head. "Not me. When I get my revenge I'll think of something better than plastic vomit."

Ben finished dressing and slammed his locker shut. "I'd love to stay and see how this big mystery ends," he said sarcastically. "But I'm out of here."

"Come out for a burger with us," Kyle suggested.

"I can't," said Ben. "I'm meeting Al at the gym."

Hoisting his gym bag over his shoulder, Ben pushed through the locker room door and onto the school parking lot. It was almost dark out. He started his car and headed for the gym.

At the first red light Ben looked in his rearview mirror. A red Triumph was speeding toward him. It looked as if it wasn't going to stop. Without thinking Ben found himself bracing for the crash—and then the driver slammed on the brakes, just in time. The driver stuck his hand out the window and waved at Ben.

Ben stared into the mirror to see the face of the driver. He breathed a sigh of relief when he recognized Bobby. He waved back.

26

The light turned green, and Ben went through the intersection. Bobby stayed close behind him—too close. Ben thought it must be a joke, but he sped up anyway. The Triumph stayed right on his tail. Ben went faster, and Bobby kept pace, honking his horn.

What's he doing? Ben thought irritably. I'm not in the mood for this.

At the next red light, Bobby pulled up beside him on the two-lane road. He revved his engine and grinned at Ben. Ben rolled down his window. "What's the big idea?" he shouted. But Bobby just kept grinning and nodding. Ben motioned for him to roll down his window, but just then the light turned green. Bobby peeled out in front of Ben and cut him off.

"That jerk," Ben muttered under his breath. "I'll show him." This time he sped up to tailgate Bobby, but Bobby suddenly slowed down. Ben slammed on his brakes. He missed Bobby's car by inches.

All right, Ben thought. If he's going to play that game, I'll just pass him.

Ben checked the left lane for oncoming cars—all clear. He darted into the lane, thinking to pass Bobby easily. But the Triumph suddenly accelerated. Ben tried to overtake it, but the red car kept just ahead of him. They were racing.

Ben slammed on his accelerator, but Bobby wouldn't let him back into the right lane. Then a bright light flooded Ben's vision.

27

A truck was coming from the other direction—right for Ben.

His heart pounding, Ben punched his horn. Bobby's car blocked the right lane. Ben was trapped.

All he saw were the huge headlights. They were heading straight for him. . . .

# CHAPTER 7

Ben covered his face with his arms, waiting for the impact. Waiting for the horrible sound and then . . .

It never came.

He opened his eyes to find himself in a bushy ditch by the side of the road. The truck tore past harmlessly, its horn blaring.

Ben dropped his head to the steering wheel, trying to catch his breath. He heard a car pull up beside him—the red Triumph.

"Ben!" Ben lifted his head. Bobby pulled the car door open on Ben's side. "That was amazing! I've never seen anybody with your nerve before."

Ben choked back a protest. Nerve?

"That must have been the thrill of your life," Bobby went on.

"I wasn't exactly thinking of it that way," Ben said. "Why wouldn't you let me back into the lane?"

"I tried to, man! But you kept copying every move I made. I slowed down, you slowed down. I sped up, you sped up. I thought you were playing with me." He slapped Ben on the back. "I've never seen anybody play a game of chicken that close. It was unbelievable."

Ben's head was reeling. A game of chicken? Was that what it was?

"Let's get to the gym now," Bobby said, moving toward his car. "And no funny stuff this time. You practically gave me a heart attack!"

Ben eased his car back onto the road. Al's a strange guy, he thought. Is there more to him than I realized?

Ben's a lucky guy, Bobby thought as he drove, slowly now, down the winding two-lane road. But so am I. I'm glad the truck didn't hit him. That would have been rushing things. I got a little carried away.

Ben isn't scared enough yet. Not nearly scared enough.

"I shouldn't be here," Ben said a couple of nights later as he glared through the smoky haze at the roadies who were setting up the stage at the nightclub.

"We know," Kyle said.

Megan, who was standing on Ben's other side,

30

reached for his hand and led him toward a table where Al was already sitting. "You need a break from schoolwork and practice," she told Ben.

No kidding, he thought. He couldn't even remember what it felt like *not* to be exhausted. Between baseball practice, school, games, homework, and working out at the gym, Ben rarely had free time. It wasn't fair to Megan, he knew, and that was the only reason he'd agreed to come to this club—so she'd have a good time. As for him, what he really wanted to do was sleep.

"Tomorrow's Sunday," Bobby said. "You don't have to get up early."

"Of course I have to get up early," Ben snapped. "Sunday and every day I get up at five-thirty, get dressed, eat breakfast, and then I practice until seven-fifteen." And it's all for nothing, he added silently. Though no one else would admit it, his pitching slump seemed to be getting worse by the day.

Bobby gave a low whistle. "I believe in 'no pain, no gain' and all that, but that sounds like one brutal regimen."

Ben put his head down on the table. "Tell that to my father."

"What's he got to do with it?" Bobby asked.

"Everything," Megan said angrily.

Ben sat up. "Let's not get into it," he said. He looked at the stage and then at his watch. It was nearly ten and the roadies were *still* setting up instruments and running sound checks. "When is the band supposed to go on?" he asked irritably. "Tomorrow?"

Meg winced as a Red Hot Chili Peppers song began to play through the huge speakers.

"Not a good sign," Bobby said solemnly. "It probably means the band's tour bus took a wrong turn and is currently stuck in traffic in New Jersey."

A slow ballad played next, and Kyle asked Meg if she wanted to dance. Meg looked at Ben questioningly. "Go ahead," he told her, mostly because if she asked *him* to dance, he'd probably fall asleep on his feet.

Ben watched as Kyle and Meg stepped out onto the floor with their arms around each other.

"She's some dancer," Bobby said.

Ben nodded. "She likes to move." He tried to ignore the fact that she and Kyle were dancing closer now, moving perfectly in sync.

Bobby leaned his chair back so that it was balancing on the back legs. "Looks like they've been practicing."

"They haven't," Ben snapped, annoyed that Al was thinking the same thing he was. He didn't like the way Kyle was looking at Meg or the way she was looking back at Kyle.

"You sure Kyle's your friend?"

"Kyle's okay," Ben replied. "We've known each other for years."

As if sensing that Ben wanted to change the subject, Bobby said, "So what exactly do you do at this sunrise practice?"

Ben shrugged. "My father and I pitch each other balls or work on hitting. He was in the minors when he was in his twenties, and he's still got a sharp eye. He says compared to the way he used to practice, I'm lazy."

"No way," Bobby said.

"Way," Ben joked.

"Why do you put up with that?"

"Put up with it?" Ben looked surprised. "I'm grateful for it. He doesn't have to get up that early. He does it for me."

Bobby took off his glasses for a moment and rubbed the bridge of his nose. Ben looked at him curiously. He had a strange feeling of déjà vu. Have I met Al somewhere before? he wondered. The thought flitted briefly through his mind, then disappeared.

The ballad ended and Ben's eyes returned to the dance floor. It had been a few minutes since he last saw Meg and Kyle. " 'Scuse me," he said, standing up.

"Where you going?" Bobby asked.

Ben's reply was terse. "To find Megan."

Bobby watched Ben work his way through the crowded floor. A minute after Ben left, Megan appeared, threading her way through the crowd toward Bobby.

"What happened to Kyle?" Bobby asked.

"He's on the prowl for a date of his own," Megan replied, smiling. "What happened to Ben?"

"I think he's looking for you."

Megan looked at the crowd and laughed. "Then we'll never find each other. *Everyone* got up to dance for that last number, everyone except you and Ben, that is."

Bobby shrugged, wondering if there was an invitation in her words. "I'm not much of a dancer," he said.

"That's what Ben always says. Come on." She tugged on his hand and he let himself be pulled to his feet. "Just this one dance," she said. "The song's almost half over. I promise, it won't be painful."

"I—" Bobby started to object, but Meg was pulling him out onto the floor. Soon they were in the middle of a wriggling mass of bodies. The music was so loud that Bobby felt each bass thump in his chest. He had never liked dancing. He could never shake that self-conscious feeling of watching himself as he moved.

"I'm a little worried about Ben," he told her, dancing halfheartedly.

She nodded. "This next week is make or break for him," she said. "The scout from Stanford is coming to Friday's game, and he's terrified that if he loses another one, they'll change their mind about the scholarship. And on top of that, he's got a ton of homework."

"Besides the English paper?" Bobby asked. Ben had been talking about his English paper when they were at the gym that afternoon.

Meg nodded again. She spun in place, a graceful whirl as the song came to a close. An announcement over the PA system said that the band would open their set in ten minutes.

"About time," Bobby said, heading back to their table.

"At least Ben's English paper is finished," Megan said. "I'm taking his disk home tonight to print it out for him—his printer is so old. But he's still got a couple of tests to study for."

Bobby shook his head. "Poor guy. No wonder he's so wired. What he needs is a good party."

Megan glanced quickly over her shoulder. Bobby looked too. No sign of Ben yet.

"What do you mean?" Megan asked.

What *do* I mean? Bobby asked himself. And then he had it—a plan that would draw Megan and Kyle together, and drive Ben totally insane. "Maybe we should throw a surprise party for Ben," Bobby said. "You know—to celebrate his scholarship and all."

"That's a fabulous idea!" Meg said. "Only where? My house is too small, and Ben's father would never approve of it at their house—"

"I bet I could ask the guys at the gym and we could hold it there," Bobby said. "I'd need you and Kyle to invite Ben's friends from school, though, and maybe help with the food. You think you two could get together and work out that part?"

"Definitely." Meg's smile was dazzling. "There's Kyle, by the stage. I'll ask him if we can get together Monday afternoon. I'll be right back."

"I'm going to look for Ben. I'll catch up with you in about ten minutes," Bobby said. He ran toward the door. Meg had just given him the *perfect* plan.

"Ben, we can't leave now," Megan protested. "The band is about to come on."

Ben gave her a weary look. "Look, Meg, I'm sorry, but I don't think I can stay awake through the first set. If you want to stay—"

"*There* you are!" Bobby interrupted. "I've been looking all over for you, man!"

"Listen, Al, would you mind staying with Megan? I'm really beat. I can't wait for this band any longer," Ben continued.

Bobby almost laughed aloud. Ben leaving his girlfriend with him! Too bad he had other things on his mind.

"It's a tempting offer," Bobby said, smiling at Megan, "but I'm pretty beat too. Maybe we should all call it a night."

Ben threw him a grateful look.

That's right, Bobby thought. I'm your friend, Ben. Trust me.

"Neither of you is any fun," Megan said crossly, but she put on her coat. Together they made their way through the crowd. The band had just started to play when they emerged from the club into the quiet spring night.

"See you day after tomorrow at the gym," Bobby called out as Ben and Meg headed for Ben's car. But instead of getting into his own rented red Triumph, he stood waiting. It took a few moments longer than he'd planned, but then he heard it: the sound of a car door opening, followed by Ben's muffled curse. And then Ben's voice, broken. "I'm dead," he cried. "I'm a dead man!"

That's right, Bobby thought. You got it.

# CHAPTER 8

"I can't believe it!" Ben moaned. He couldn't remember ever having felt so out of control in his life. "I am dead. I am absolutely, totally dead!"

"You're not dead," Meg said reasonably. "Just stay calm. I'm sure we'll find it."

Ben refused to calm down. "My window's been smashed. The tape deck's gone. My knapsack's gone—" His body tensed as he heard the sound of footsteps running toward them, then relaxed as he realized it was just Al.

"What's wr—" Bobby began, and then stopped himself as he took in the damage. "Someone really did a number on your car."

"Tell me something I don't know," Ben said, wishing he'd never left his house that evening.

What was he thinking about, driving around with his whole life in the backseat of his car?

Bobby peered into the car's dark interior. "What did they get?"

"His tape deck," Megan answered.

"I don't care about that!" Ben said, his voice rising. "They took my knapsack! They took my knapsack!"

"So? What was in there?" Bobby asked.

"His wallet," Megan answered. "I'll go call the police."

"My English paper is gone," Ben said grimly.

"It's all right, Ben," Megan said. "Can't we just print out another copy?"

"You don't understand," Ben said impatiently. "It was on a floppy disk, in my knapsack. I don't have a hard copy. Now the disk is gone—and I haven't got another copy!"

"Okay, hold on," Bobby said, moving slowly around the car. "Whoever did this doesn't want your homework. That's for sure. They probably took the money and ditched the knapsack somewhere nearby . . ."

But after searching the parking lot and nearby garbage cans, they had found nothing. The police had already come and gone, and they had been little help.

Ben stared at the ground, feeling sick to his stomach.

"It's going to be all right," Megan said. "I bet you can reconstruct most of your paper from memory."

Ben gave her an angry look. "The quotes? The footnotes? You know how long all that took me?"

Megan looked down. "I know."

"Ben," Bobby broke in gently, "this isn't Megan's fault."

Ben felt his anger fade. "No, you're right, it isn't." He walked over to Megan and put his arm around her. "Sorry," he told her. "This is just the last thing I needed right now."

"Don't worry about it." She hugged him back and smiled at him. "C'mon, we better go. The sooner you start trying to put the paper back together, the better."

Ben let out a long sigh. "Okay," he said. He started back toward his car. Then he turned to Bobby. "What about you?"

"In a minute," Bobby said. "I want to look around a little more. The guy who stole your backpack could have dropped it a few blocks away."

"Thanks," Ben said. "Don't look too long."

"I won't," Bobby promised.

Ben brushed the shards of broken glass from the seat and then he and Megan got into the car. "It's going to be a cold ride home without a windshield," he told her. "Maybe I should ask Al to take you home."

"No way," Megan said, taking his hand in hers.

They rode in silence for a few minutes. Then Megan said, "Your paper will write itself. I'll even come over and help you."

"That would be great," said Ben. "We could make a study date for Monday afternoon."

Meg didn't answer. Ben began to wonder if she'd heard him. "Hello?" he said, taking his eyes off the road again. "Anybody home?"

"I can't Monday afternoon."

"Why not?"

"Uh . . . I have to do some . . . tutoring . . . some sixth graders are coming over to my house. Problem readers."

He threw her another look. But she just smiled. "Everything is going to work out, I promise," she said.

She was right, he knew. So why didn't he feel as confident as she sounded?

Bobby had promised Ben he wouldn't search too long for his missing knapsack. He kept his promise. As soon as Ben's car was out of sight, he headed back to his Triumph and removed the knapsack from the trunk. He left the tape deck inside—he'd sell that later. Going to the nearest trash can, he took Ben's disk from the knapsack.

Don't worry about your English paper, Ben, he thought. That's easily taken care of. By the time I'm done with you you'll wish all your troubles were so easy to cure.

Then Bobby took a pocket knife out of his pocket and slowly, carefully . . . he cut Ben's disk into tiny pieces and tossed them into the garbage.

"Disk error," he said to himself, laughing at his own private joke.

41

# CHAPTER 9

When the phone rang later that night, Ben answered it on the first ring.

"Hey, Ben, it's Al."

"Hi. What's up?"

"I found it, but you guys took off before I came back." Bobby said. "I found the knapsack."

Ben's heart soared. "You're kidding!" But there was silence at the other end of the line. And then Ben realized that Al didn't sound excited at all, and that meant bad news.

"It's empty," Bobby said quietly. "A couple of pencils in the pocket, that's about it."

"Great!" Ben said. "Now I'll be up all night for sure. I had about six solid days of work in that paper, and now I've got until Tuesday morning to try and put it all together again."

There was a pause. Then Bobby said, "Listen, I could make some phone calls."

"Huh?"

"You know, I could call some of my friends in college. I know a bunch of guys who are good in English. They've probably all written the same paper you're working on."

Ben smiled. He could still get out of this mess. "Yeah?" Then he checked himself. "That's really nice of you, but I'd never—"

"No, I know, I know," Bobby said quickly. "I just thought, if you get really stuck . . . and you want to rest up this week 'cause of the game coming up with the Stanford scout and all."

Ben took a deep breath. It'd be a miracle if he managed to survive this week, let alone get enough sleep and play a good game. "Look," he said, "I appreciate the offer, but—"

"Hey, I'm not suggesting you copy anyone else's work," Bobby protested. "I just thought maybe I could call my friends and they could give you a few ideas. Listen," he went on, "I'll bring the knapsack with me when I pick you up Monday afternoon. We're still working out on Monday, aren't we?"

"Of course."

"Good. In the meantime, try to get some sleep."

"Yeah, right," Ben said.

As he sat back down to work he thought about Al finding his knapsack and offering to help with ideas for the Poe paper. Al was a hard guy to figure out. He'd turned out to be a great partner for co-training, but in all the time they'd worked out together he'd never told Ben much about himself.

And even though he was at least a year older, he seemed to like hanging out with Ben's friends. Megan liked him, and she was a pretty good judge of people. Then again, lately Megan seemed a little too interested in other guys . . .

Early Monday afternoon, before he picked up Ben for the gym, Bobby drove to the Middletown Public Library.

Twenty minutes later, he had what he wanted —an essay on Poe by some big-shot professor at Harvard. With the book propped up before him on the desk in the main reading room, he started typing into his laptop.

He was typing word for word.

When he was finished, he took the paper and got into his car. He opened the glove compartment and took out a small vial. The pale yellow liquid gleamed in the sunlight.

Acid.

Bobby smiled.

Yes, I'm going to kill you, Ben Douglas, he said to himself. But first you're going to feel a little pain.

Ben was the first to get to the gym before practice that afternoon. He walked into the empty locker room and sat down hard on one of the wooden benches that lined the wall.

If only I didn't have practice today, I'd have

more time to rewrite my paper, he thought wearily. But I can't miss practice. I've got to get back on track. If I win this game on Friday, he thought, that could make up for everything.

He grimaced as he lifted his right arm—his pitching arm. It ached. He reached for the muscle liniment.

He opened the jar and started rubbing the white cream on his arm. He felt the nice comforting warmth of the cream going into his muscles.

Then the liniment burned. "Ow," Ben said aloud. It had never been quite this hot before.

His arm and hand felt as if they were on fire!

# CHAPTER 10

**B**en screamed in pain. He looked at his arm and screamed again, a hoarse, horrible cry.

The skin on his arm began to bubble and blister.

The pain was unbearable. His arm burned and burned.

He ran to the sink and splashed cold water on his arm, desperately trying to stop the burning.

But nothing he did made it stop. The pain shot through his arm and flooded his brain until he could stand it no longer.

He collapsed in a heap on the floor.

Ben came to a few minutes later. His arm was beginning to feel better. Coach Warner was rubbing something cool and soothing on it.

"What happened?" asked Ben.

The coach frowned. "You boys have carried this practical joking too far." He wrapped Ben's arm in a bandage. "Better skip practice today, Ben."

"But, Coach—"

"You heard me. Go home and rest. You'll be all right tomorrow."

At ten of five that afternoon, Ben stood waiting outside his house. Right on time, the red Triumph turned the corner.

"Hop in," Bobby said cheerfully. "Whoa, you look awful."

Ben looked up with a weak smile. "Thanks a lot."

Bobby nodded toward Ben's bandaged right arm. "What happened?"

"Some joker put acid in my liniment."

Bobby gasped. "Who would do something like that?"

Right away Ben's mind went to Kyle. All those practical jokes in the locker room . . . and Meg . . .

He couldn't imagine Kyle doing something like that. But who else had a reason to?

"Are you sure you want to work out?" Bobby asked.

"It's all right. It burned like crazy for a while, but the coach put some salve on it and bandaged it up. It's not the arm that bothers me—"

"Something else on your mind?"

"It's Megan. I'm sure it's nothing, but I tried to

47

call her just now. And Saturday she said she couldn't get together this afternoon because she was going to be home tutoring, but . . ."

"But what?"

"This is so stupid. She wasn't there, that's all. She wasn't home like she said she would be."

"Oh," said Bobby. "That *is* nothing. She probably ended up tutoring at the kids' house. Or maybe you misunderstood her."

"Right."

Ben glanced out at the intersection they were passing. "Aren't we going to the gym?"

Bobby looked at him strangely, as if he didn't understand, then looked back at the road. "Did I mess up? Don't we turn right on Mulholland?"

"No, you turned left on Mulholland," Ben pointed out to him.

Bobby blew out a short irritated breath. "I'm such an idiot."

Ben yawned. "It's okay," he mumbled. "Just go straight. We can go around the traffic circle."

"I've got a lousy sense of direction," Bobby said apologetically. "This is really the long way around, isn't it?"

"Don't worry about it." Ben suddenly sat up, his eyes wide. "Slow down a minute," he ordered.

"Why?"

"Just do it."

Bobby slowed the Triumph, traveling slowly along a street lined with split-level houses. "This scenery's not that exciting," he said doubtfully.

"Yeah, it is," Ben replied through his teeth. He

nodded toward a white house with red trim. "That's Kyle's house, and that's Meg's blue car parked right in front of it."

"Are you sure?"

"Of course, I am. I'd know her car anywhere."

"Does Horner tutor too?" Bobby asked innocently as he drove on.

"What? No, no . . ." Ben could feel the fear and then the anger start to bubble up inside him. What was Meg doing with Kyle? He knew there was something odd about her tutoring story, but he hadn't expected this.

"Forget about it," Bobby said. "You'll find out what it was next time you talk to her. I'm sure it's nothing."

Ben didn't answer.

"Well, listen," Bobby said. "I brought your knapsack, and I've got a surprise for you. Maybe this will cheer you up." As he drove, he reached behind him and fumbled around on the backseat. "Ta-da!" he said, pulling his hand back. He was holding a paper. "Take it," he told Ben.

Ben looked at the paper in Bobby's hand and felt his heart skip a beat. "The Theme of Guilt from Past Crimes in the Works of Edgar Allan Poe," read the title, "by Ben Douglas."

"Where did this come from?" he asked.

"I called around. You didn't think I'd let you down, did you?"

"I appreciate the thought, Al, but—"

Bobby didn't let him finish. "My friend Pete had this paper on Poe from first semester. He got a

49

B on it, so he saved it. I just retyped the first page with your name on it."

"You've got to be kidding," he said.

"I'm totally serious. Your problems are answered, my friend."

"I can't."

"Sure you can. It's easy. Just take it," Bobby coaxed. "Then you can get some sleep tonight and still turn in your paper tomorrow. Friday is coming, Ben."

Ben looked at the paper in Bobby's hand. It was so tempting. It was also cheating, and he'd never cheated in his life.

"It's a dumb idea," he told Bobby angrily. "I can't risk getting caught with something like this."

"Caught?" Bobby laughed. "Do you know how many students write papers on Poe every year? This is one of *thousands*. No one's ever going to know it's not yours unless you tell them."

"It's not right," Ben said stubbornly.

"Look," Bobby said, "everyone who knows you, knows you're not the kind of guy to cheat. Cutting yourself a little slack *just this once* so you can win that game on Friday isn't going to change that."

Ben shook his head, trying to clear it. Why did everything seem so confusing lately? It used to be that he knew exactly where he stood. Only a few weeks ago he was a top high school athlete with good grades and a beautiful girlfriend who loved him. Now all of those certainties were slipping away.

Bobby set the paper down alongside the stick shift. "Do what you think is best," he said. "Just remember. A paper on Poe is already written and even typed, and sitting right here. All you have to do is take it."

Ben closed his eyes, not answering. But Bobby's words echoed through his mind: "All you have to do is take it."

"Al" was right. All he had to do was take it.

# CHAPTER 11

Ben stretched as Bobby parked the Triumph across the street from the gym. He grabbed his gym bag from the back, started out of the car, and then stopped. "Al" hadn't said another word about his friend's Poe essay, but Ben hadn't been able to stop thinking about it. It couldn't hurt to take the paper, he reasoned. He didn't have to turn it in or even copy it. Maybe he could just read it over for some ideas. He reached back into the car and his hand closed over the paper.

"Smart move," Bobby said.

Ben felt his face flush. "I guess it'll be okay this once." He quickly stuffed the essay into his backpack. "Thanks."

Bobby slapped him on the back. "That's one worry off your mind, right?"

But by the time he got back from the gym an hour and a half later, Ben was feeling even more worried and pressured. All he could think about was Megan's car parked in front of Kyle's house.

He headed straight for the kitchen. He grabbed a Coke from the fridge and had just started making himself a sandwich when the phone rang. He picked up the red wall phone next to the kitchen table.

"It's me," said a girl's voice.

"Meg!" he said, glad to hear her voice. Then he remembered seeing her car at Kyle's. "What's going on?" he asked, his voice cool.

"Oh, nothing much. I'm pretty tired."

"Yeah? Why's that?"

"Ben, are you okay? You sound—I don't know—you sound strange."

"I'm fine. So how did it go this afternoon?"

"How did what go?"

"You were tutoring some sixth graders. Remember?"

"Oh, right. I just didn't know what you were talking about for a second. It went fine."

Ben's heart was pounding. He tried to keep his voice casual. "You tutored them at your house?"

"Uh-huh," she said.

Ben waited. There was a long pause.

"Are you sure you're okay?" Meg asked again.

"Are you sure you were at your house this afternoon?" he shot back.

"All right," she said. "Let's have it. What's going on?"

"I saw your car parked outside Kyle's house. Don't tell me you weren't there."

There was an endless silence at the other end of the line. Finally Meg spoke, "Ben, I can explain—"

"I thought we trusted each other," he cut her off. "I thought—"

"Ben, wait a minute." Meg was laughing. "I'm flattered and all that you're jealous, but this is all a big misunderstanding."

"You got that right!"

"No, no, listen. I can explain everything. But not . . . right now."

"Oh, that's very comforting."

"Ben," Megan said. She wasn't laughing anymore. "I'm serious. There is no problem, okay? Just take my word for it."

Ben felt himself shaking with cold fury. "You lied to me," he said. "That's a problem. No matter what the explanation is, I don't like being lied to."

"I didn't lie to you," she said quietly. "Not like you think."

"How can you say that?"

"I'm saying it."

He shook his head in disbelief. "You're too much, you know that?"

"You don't really trust me, do you?"

"I trust you," Ben said reluctantly, "but it's hard when—" He stopped, not even sure of what he was accusing her of. Did he really believe Meg was seeing Kyle behind his back? It just wasn't like her. "Meg," he said gently, "this is getting way out of hand."

"I guess it is," she agreed.

He sank down in the chair beneath the phone, relaxing for the first time since the conversation began. Everything was going to be okay, after all. "Look, I know you have a good explanation for why you were at Kyle's," he said. "So just tell me now. What's the big deal?"

The silence at the other end of the line made his scalp prickle. "You want to know right now?" Megan said suddenly. "I'm in love with Kyle Horner, okay? I want to marry him and have his kids. And if you can't figure out what we were doing this afternoon, then you get an F in Biology."

Ben felt the blood pounding into his face. "Well, then, I've got news for you. We're through!"

"I'm heartbroken, I really am," Megan replied furiously. "But I've got some news for you. You can't dump me, because I'm dumping *you*!" And with that the phone slammed in Ben's ear, and the line went dead.

"Everything okay?" his mother called in after a moment. It was several seconds before he was able to force out an unconvincing "Yeah, everything's fine, Mom."

Bobby was in the middle of a set of one-armed push-ups when he heard a soft knocking at the door of his apartment. He stopped, wondering if he was imagining it. The knock came again.

"Al?"

He crossed to the door and looked out the peephole. He blinked, not believing what he saw.

Megan was standing there. How? he asked himself. He never gave out his address to anyone. So how had she traced him? There was only one way to find out. He reached for the doorknob.

Suddenly he froze, realizing that she'd see the wall with all his clippings and photographs of the Five.

"Megan," he said through the door. "Just a second, okay? I was in the middle of working out. I'm not exactly dressed."

"I'm really sorry to bother you," she said. "But I need . . ." Her voice trailed off.

"Just give me a second," Bobby called. He was frantically pulling down the clippings.

"Should I come back another time?"

"No, no, now is fine. I'll be right"—he shoved the clippings under his mattress on the floor—"with you."

When he opened the door Megan was staring at the floor, as if she didn't want to meet his gaze. "Come on in," he said. He locked the door behind her—both locks.

"Thanks," Meg said, sounding nervous. "Sorry to barge in on you like this."

"It's okay." Placing both hands on her shoulders, he steered her gently toward the one chair in the studio. "Sit," he said. "Would you like a glass of water or something?"

"Thanks." Meg's eyes were red and puffy. "Water would be great." She looked around the bare room.

"I haven't really had time to fix it up yet," he

said, handing her a glass of water. He pointed to the milk crate beside his bed that he used as a night table. "That's as fancy as my furniture gets." He waited a few moments, giving her time to calm down, before asking, "How'd you ever find me? I don't remember giving you my address."

Megan sniffed and gave him a tremulous smile. "You didn't. I followed you."

Bobby fought down a surge of disbelief. She'd followed him and he hadn't even known it! He'd thought he was more careful than that. "So why exactly did you follow me?" he asked, trying to sound as if he thought it was amusing.

"I was just driving around and I saw your car . . . and I really needed to talk to someone so I just . . . Oh, Al, I'm so upset. The party's off. I know you're probably busy, but I really need to talk to someone—someone who knows Ben."

"What's up?" asked Bobby.

Her voice dropped so low Bobby could barely hear her. "Ben and I had a fight."

Much to his surprise Bobby found himself wanting to comfort her. "Hey, it can't be that bad," he said. "Ben's crazy about you."

"Not crazy enough. We broke up." The words themselves seemed to break something inside her, and she started to sob softly.

"I know what you need," Bobby said, his tone teasing.

"What?" she sniffed.

He picked up a sharp knife from the kitchen counter and turned toward her. Meg frowned, tilting her head to one side, her expression totally confused.

"An apple," he said, reaching into his nearly empty fridge. "It'll make you feel better. Trust me." He took a sharp knife from the kitchen counter and began slicing the apple into wedges. "So," he went on, handing her a slice, "what happened? Do you want to talk about it?"

Megan didn't answer right away. She took a slice of the apple, got up, and crossed to the window, her back to Bobby.

"You know how you suggested Kyle and I get together to work out the guest list and food? Well, I was at Kyle's house, and that was *all* we were doing, but Ben saw my car there and—and now everything's a mess."

Bobby felt a rush of pure triumph. He'd set it up perfectly.

"Ben's gotten it into his head that I'm cheating on him—with Kyle, if you can believe that," Meg went on, her back still turned. "What is his problem?"

Bobby shrugged. "Ben's been under a lot of stress lately—"

"It's just all so stupid!" she broke in. "I mean, Kyle and I were just planning a party—for him! We were just trying to do something nice. And even when the fight got bad I didn't tell Ben the truth because I figured we'd work things out, and I didn't want to ruin the surprise. But the whole thing got out of control. It was such a great idea that you had, throwing this party for Ben."

She turned suddenly, saw him clutching the knife in his fist, and started.

He laughed. He liked seeing her that way, a little scared. He cut another slice of apple and held it out to her. "Want some more?"

She shook her head and started to cry again. Clutching the knife in one hand, he stood behind her and began to massage her shoulder with the other. I could kiss her if I want, Bobby thought. I could steal her from Ben. He had planned on using Kyle to ruin Ben's relationship with Megan—it hadn't occurred to Bobby that she might actually go for *him*.

"This is all going to work out, Meg. I know it," he said soothingly. His voice became quieter. "You and Ben are going to get back together and clear this whole mess up."

Meg turned into his arms and he felt her body jerk with sobs.

"Shhh," he said gently. He lifted her chin and carefully wiped away her tears.

Another tear rolled slowly down her cheek. This one he kissed away.

His arms tightened around her, holding her close, so close he could feel every breath she took.

Bobby studied her small, perfect face and felt an unfamiliar sense of confusion. He was about to kiss her again—but he stopped. No! He had to keep his priorities straight. If he got involved with Meg, he wouldn't be able to keep his mind on Ben. He suddenly felt a surge of hatred well up inside him. He squeezed the knife in his hand.

I could kill her instead, he thought. Right here and now.

Behind her back, he raised the knife high.

It's my call whether she lives or dies, he thought, gripping the knife until his knuckles were white. Her life depends on me.

She has no idea what's going through my mind. She'd never know what hit her. . . .

Meg suddenly looked up at him and smiled.

It's my decision, he thought again.

He let her go.

She stood on tiptoe and kissed him on the cheek. "I'd better go home," she said.

"Right," he said, running his hand through his hair.

She stepped back from him, picked up her bag, and went to the door. "I'll let you know how things work out," she promised.

"You do that," Bobby said. He opened the double locks for her. "Get home safe now," he said.

"I will," she promised.

Bobby watched out the window until he was sure Meg had driven away. Then he calmly, systematically began to replace the clippings on his wall. He worked until his gallery of the Five was once more intact.

He stared at the photographs of Ben, willing himself to forget Meg. All he wanted was to feel the hatred he'd been storing up since he was twelve. He was going to murder Ben Douglas, and nothing was going to get in his way.

# CHAPTER 12

"Major game today, huh, Douglas?"

"Ace 'em, Ben!"

"Hey, Ben, you ready to waste those losers?"

It was Friday afternoon, and Ben walked through the crowded hallway at school, barely noticing his friends' comments. He was used to this sort of thing on the day of a big game. Today might be the most important game he'd ever pitched. The scout from Stanford would be there, watching him. Ben knew he had to break his losing streak if he wanted that scholarship. And all he could think about was Megan. They hadn't spoken to each other since their fight. He felt hurt, angry, and confused, all at the same time.

He stopped at the end of the hallway as he saw

a short man in a suit with a crew cut. The man was talking to one of the teachers, and the teacher was pointing at Ben. The man waved and smiled. Ben had never seen him before.

The man walked up to him and held out his hand. "Ben Douglas?"

"Yes?"

"Barry Hefflin. I'm the scouting representative from Stanford."

"Oh, yeah, hi." Ben smiled and stuck out his hand, giving the man a firm shake. Life was so weird. Ben had been looking forward to this day, this meeting, all semester. But now that it was finally happening, he felt oddly numb.

"We've heard a lot about you, Ben," the Stanford scout said. "I'm looking forward to quite a show today."

"You'll get one, sir," Ben said, trying to summon up his old confidence.

"Well," Hefflin said, "I don't want to keep you. I know you have to get ready. I—we'll speak after the game."

"Great."

Ben watched Hefflin head out the double doors, then he turned and went to his locker. Opening the narrow metal door, he stuffed his books inside with an angry motion. He'd give Hefflin a show, all right, but not the kind he expected. Ben's whole body felt heavy and achy, and the idea of actually trying to pitch a game like this was a joke. He'd barely slept all week. The nights he wasn't up working on papers or studying for tests, he'd been up worrying about Megan. He slammed his locker shut. This was ridiculous. He was going to find Meg and talk to her, work this thing out, no matter what.

If anything had happened between Meg and Kyle, it was probably Kyle's fault, he told himself. Anyway, he loved Megan. He couldn't be without her. He'd get her back—somehow. But first he had to get her away from Kyle.

He suddenly stopped short. At first he thought he was seeing things. But no. His father was walking toward him, his face ashen.

"Dad," Ben said, "what are you doing here?"

Ben felt a wave of fear go through him. Something was very wrong. "Dad, what is it? Is Mom all right?"

"Your mother's fine. The problem is you."

"Me?" Ben thought frantically, trying to figure out what was wrong.

"You have everything going for you. Everything. And you're willing to give it all up because you're too lazy to write an English paper."

Ben felt sick to his stomach.

"I just got a call from Mr. Shanley," his father went on. "He says he finished grading a paper of yours. He said it was copied from a famous essay—copied word for word."

Ben barely heard the rest of what his father was saying. ". . . plagiarism . . . a very serious offense . . . appear before the school Disciplinary Committee . . . automatic suspension . . . no way you can play in the game today or any other day . . . What do you have to say for yourself?'' his father finished.

Ben opened his mouth and found he had nothing to say. Finally, he managed, "I'm sorry, Dad. I didn't mean to let you down. I actually did it so I *wouldn't* let you down."

"That's a great excuse," said his father. "Blame it on me. I'll see you at home this afternoon. You and I are going to have a long talk."

Ben nodded and watched his father as he stormed out of the building.

He closed his eyes and leaned against his locker. He felt sick and dizzy. He couldn't imagine things being okay again. He couldn't imagine them getting any worse.

"Yo, Douglas, ready for the game?" a familiar voice asked.

Ben looked up and felt a wave of rage go through him as Kyle sauntered over.

"Get out of here," Ben said in a low voice.

Kyle sat down beside him. "What?"

"I said get out of here before I break your face."

Kyle put a hand on his back. "Hey, man, what's your problem? Hey—" He never finished his sentence. Ben lunged at him, grabbing his shirt with one hand and shoving him up against the lockers. Kyle tried to twist away but he wasn't strong enough.

Ben moved as if he were on automatic. He wasn't even aware of clenching his other fist or smashing it repeatedly into Kyle's rib cage.

All he knew was that suddenly a door

slammed. Mr. Dunn, the history teacher, was standing about six inches away, his eyes popping. "Douglas! Horner!" he roared. "Break it up!"

Ben looked down and saw that Kyle was curled up on the floor, his arms clutching his ribs.

"Horner, are you all right?" the teacher asked. "Let's get you to the nurse."

Kyle nodded and stood up, still clutching his rib cage. He gave Ben a look of anger and confusion. "There's something wrong with you, man," he said, his voice shaky.

Mr. Dunn helped Kyle down the hall. He glanced back at Ben. "I'll see you about this later, Douglas."

It doesn't matter, Ben thought hopelessly. It doesn't matter what you have to say to me, Mr. Dunn. My whole life is over anyway.

# CHAPTER 13

T he phone started ringing almost as soon as he got home. Ben really couldn't deal with this right now. His parents weren't home yet, and he wasn't in the mood to talk to anyone. He walked through the kitchen, dumped his books on a chair, and went upstairs to his room. The phone was still ringing. He sat on his bed and picked it up.

"Hello," he said dully.

"Ben, it's Al."

Ben didn't respond.

Bobby asked, "You there?"

"Uh-huh."

"Listen, I heard . . . I'm sorry, man. I had no idea about the plagiarism thing."

"Uh-huh," Ben said again.

"I just can't believe this," Bobby said.

66

"Me neither."

"No, I mean, I trusted Pete. He told me he had written that paper himself."

"I trusted you," Ben said.

"I know," Bobby said. "I'm—I'm sorry. But I'm going to find a way to straighten this all out, I promise."

"There is no way."

"I just can't believe Pete would do something like this," Bobby said. "Pete is—"

"Listen," Ben interrupted. "I don't really care about Pete, if you want to know the truth. What I care about is now I'm going to get kicked out of school. I'm going to lose my scholarship. I'm going to lose everything."

"Well," Bobby said, "if you're going to think like that, you will."

"What do you mean?"

"Look, I know this English paper business is a mess. But you can get out of anything. Anything. Don't start talking like a loser."

Ben felt a red wave of anger go through him. "Oh, right. This is all an attitude problem. I'll be expelled, Al. This is the end of the line for me."

Bobby was silent for a moment before saying, "There's no situation that can't be handled."

"Thanks for the brilliant advice," Ben snapped, and started to hang up.

"Wait a minute," Bobby said.

"I'm hanging up now," Ben shot back.

"Go ahead," Bobby said. "Get mad at me all you like. You can even try to convince yourself that this is all my fault. You're letting them hold this scholarship over your head like a guillotine."

"My scholarship matters," Ben said.

"Only if you let it. You're making it the most important thing in your life, and there are plenty of other things you can do."

"Oh, give me a break!" Ben nearly yelled.

"You're scared of a bunch of teachers and terrified of your father," Bobby taunted. "What's wrong? Is Daddy going to be disappointed?"

"You—" Ben began.

"You are such a poser," Bobby went on. "Middletown High's Golden Boy—watch him collapse. Things get a little rough, and the only thing he knows how to do is panic."

Ben grit his teeth. "I know how to out-muscle you."

Bobby laughed. "Right."

"Any place, any time, you understand?"

Bobby yawned.

"What? You don't think I can?"

"I thought we were cotraining," Bobby said. "I didn't know we were competing."

"Fine, I'm competing," Ben said angrily. "And I'm going to leave you in the dust."

"You're losing it, Ben."

"I'm losing it? You're the one who's going to lose." Bobby didn't answer, which made Ben even angrier. "How about right now?" Ben said. "Let's go down to the gym right now."

"C'mon, Ben, get serious. It's after nine."

68

"I'm totally serious. We have keys. What difference does it make what time it is?"

There was a pause. "Okay," Bobby said finally. "You're on."

Bobby smirked as he hung up the telephone. It was almost too easy, but he wasn't going to give up this chance. He's ready, he thought, anticipation rising up within him. Ben's time has come at last.

# CHAPTER 14

The lights were on in the gym when Ben arrived. The front door was open and Bobby was inside. Ben found him wearing his street clothes and weight-lifting gloves, stretching out on the mats.

"Listen," Ben said as he set his bag down on the floor. "I'm half out of my mind. We don't have to do this. I'm just mad at you about the essay."

"You challenged me," Bobby said in a steely voice. "And that means we're on, Douglas. I'm going to prove it to you once and for all."

Bobby had turned on a few lights, but the deserted gym still looked eerie and dark. "Come on," Ben said. "I don't want to fight with you. Let's just forget about this and go home."

"But you want to fight it out, don't you? You

70

think you can beat me, when it comes down to it, don't you?"

"All right," Ben said. "Sure. I'm the star super jock." He shook his head and gave a hollow laugh. "I've even got a room full of trophies to prove it."

"Then why are you so afraid to prove it here?"

Ben sighed. "Al—"

"You're something else, Douglas," Bobby said. "You drag me down here, you brag about how easily you can beat me, and the moment you get here, you start trying to get out of it."

"I'm not trying to get out—"

Bobby gave Ben a hard shove with the heel of his hand.

"Okay," Ben said. No one pushed him around and got away with it. "Let's do it." He gazed around the room at the exercise equipment. "How do you want to work this?"

"The Smith machine," Bobby said grimly. "You bench press as much as you can. Then I'll do ten pounds more."

"Ten reps?" Ben asked.

"Ten reps."

They moved to the bench press without looking at each other.

"How much weight you want?" Bobby asked quietly.

"Two-fifty."

"Get real," Bobby said. "That's pushing Olympic."

Ben bent down and started loading the free weights onto the barbell.

"Is this some kind of joke?" Bobby asked. "You're just going to humiliate yourself and get hurt."

"Don't bet on it," Ben shot back. He got himself into position, fastening the seat belt. "What's wrong? Afraid you can't do two-sixty?"

Bobby crossed his arms over his chest. "You're the one who's going to lose. All set?" Bobby smiled down at him, a strange smile.

"Let's go," Ben said.

Bobby twisted the barbell so the hooks came off the frame. Ben grunted and barely managed to slow the barbell as it came down. He took a deep breath, exhaled, and pushed with all his strength. But he couldn't raise the barbell back up. Then he realized why. Bobby was holding it down.

"Who's the loser now?" Bobby asked softly.

Ben struggled futilely to lift the weight. Finally, he said, "Okay, okay, I lose. Hook it into the frame."

"Hook what?" Bobby asked with mock innocence.

"Cut the games!" Ben snapped. "Get this thing off me."

Keeping his weight on the barbell, Bobby bent down. He picked up another five-pound weight. "I don't know what's wrong with my hearing. I really didn't hear what you said. What do you want me to do? Add more weight?"

"That's not funny," Ben said.

"Sorry," Bobby said. Then he slid the weight onto one end of the barbell.

Ben felt himself beginning to panic. "What are you doing? I said take the weight off!"

"What's the matter, Ben? You feeling . . . scared?"

Every muscle in Ben's body was trembling. Bobby picked up another five-pound weight. He hefted it in his hand. Then he placed the black weight on the other end of the barbell.

*"Are you insane?"*

"Probably," Bobby said. "But if I am, you made me that way." He carefully slid another weight onto the barbell. "See, I keep wondering when you'll remember me, Ben. But I guess I never meant that much to you. I guess you never noticed the people around you, even when you were destroying their lives."

He added another weight. Ben's eyes were bulging with strain. But he was trying desperately to make sense out of what Al was telling him. Remember him?

"My name's not Al, Ben. It's Bobby. Bobby Wimmer? The Whitlock Mansion. Remember, Ben? Your little test? I just wanted to be part of your group."

Ben strained against the weight, but he was also remembering. Now he knew what it was he hadn't been seeing. The twelve-year-old runty kid who had straggled after the Five. Making him run through the old mansion. He had fallen. Ben had felt terrible. Especially when the kid had spent time in the hospital. But then the boy had moved away and—

Bobby Wimmer. Ben stared up into his face with horror. But that boy—he could see him now—that boy had brown hair.

"I look different?" Bobby said. "I know. The hair's dyed, the glasses are fake."

"Please, Bobby," Ben pleaded. "Let me up. I've always felt bad about that day. I . . . really have. C'mon—take this thing off me—and—we'll talk."

Bobby only laughed. He lifted another weight, a ten-pound weight.

"No, no, no!" cried Ben.

"Ooh," said Bobby. "Listen to little Ben. He's whimpering!"

As Ben begged, Bobby began to hum. "Scared to death, scared to death, little Ben is scared to death . . ."

Still humming, he slowly slipped the ten-pound weight into position—

And Ben finally realized he was going to die. . . .

# CHAPTER 15

Bobby added one more weight. Then one more. Ben's arms gave out at last. The huge barbell crashed down onto his chest and Ben gave a dull moan.

With his gloved hands, Bobby rolled the barbell a few inches backward onto Ben's throat. He was sort of sorry when Ben stopped making choking sounds. The show was over.

Bobby cleared his wall once again, taking special pleasure in taking down the photographs of Ben Douglas. Carefully, he put all of his clippings of the Five in a suitcase, covered them with his few articles of clothing, and left the key to the apartment on the kitchen table. He was done with Middletown for a while.

Megan was going to be upset, he realized. He hadn't wanted to upset her. For a while there, he even thought about letting Ben live. He was having so much fun playing with him—the essay, the acid, playing chicken in the car—it was almost enough.

But then Ben had acted so sure of himself, like he was still king of the school, and he knew that Ben hadn't changed. He knew that Ben had to die.

His mind went back to Megan. She was smart. She knew where this place was, which was why he had to leave without a trace. He really shouldn't take chances. He really ought to kill her before he left town.

He picked up the kitchen knife. For Meg, he'd make it quick. None of the drawn-out terror he'd planned for the Five. Then again, Meg hadn't been like the Five. She was nice to him. He liked her.

Bobby took a quarter out of his pocket, flipped it, and covered it with his palm. "We're gonna leave it to fate, Meg," he said softly. "Heads, you live. Tails, you die."

He uncovered the coin and smiled.

"Lucky girl."

# CHAPTER 16

Carlyn Alexander sat on the window seat of her dorm room, staring at the people passing through the quad. She'd been thinking about Jamie, and about Leigh's murder. The case was still unsolved, and this nagged at Carlyn.

I bet Jamie never called Ben Douglas, she thought. But I'm sure he must know something. After all, he lives right across the street from the Millens. Maybe he remembers somebody from Middletown who might have had a grudge against them.

She went to the phone and called Middletown information. A moment later, she was dialing Ben's number.

On the fourth ring, a man's voice answered.

"Mr. Douglas?" she began. "This is an old

friend of Ben's, Carlyn Alexander. Is he there?" Silence. "Mr. Douglas?"

The voice that finally answered her was strained, horrible. "Ben's dead," he said.

Carlyn felt as if she had just been kicked in the stomach. "What?"

"He went to the gym . . . by himself . . . a terrible accident . . ." Before Carlyn could think of anything else to ask or say, there was a quiet click. Mr. Douglas had hung up.

Carlyn sat shaking on the window seat. Ben was dead.

Leigh. And now Ben.

Carlyn walked into her dorm room, dropped her suitcase on the floor, and sank down on her bed without even taking off her coat. She was completely drained. It was nearly ten at night. That morning at nine she'd gone to Ben Douglas's funeral. Since about two that afternoon she'd been making her way back to Indiana via train. The trains had been delayed, of course, not to mention so crowded that she'd had to stand the entire time. Altogether, it had been the worst day of her life—except for the day of Leigh's funeral.

Carlyn stared up at the ceiling and then shut her eyes. She felt numb and sick. And she was still reeling with disbelief. Everyone in Middletown, including the police, said that Ben's death was an accident. He'd gone in to use the equipment unsupervised and taken on more weight than he could handle.

It didn't make sense to Carlyn. Ben had been strong and athletic, but he wasn't a giant—why would he even try to lift a barbell with that much weight on it?

Carlyn sat up unhappily. She might as well take her coat off and unpack. And then she'd better get some sleep. Tomorrow morning she had an eight A.M. organic chemistry lecture.

Poor Ben, Carlyn thought miserably. She couldn't shake the image of Megan, pale and grief-stricken, crying, "Please, no!" as the casket was lowered into the ground.

After the funeral at the Douglases' house Megan had been calmer. She and Carlyn had talked for a while. Megan had told Carlyn that in the weeks before his death Ben had had a run of really rotten luck. Lots of things had gone wrong. She added that Ben had made a new friend, Al Dalton, who hadn't been seen since the day Ben died. Megan had tried to call Al, had even gone to his apartment, but he seemed to have disappeared.

Carlyn had thought this Al sounded very suspicious. She had called the police and asked if they had checked him out, but they said they didn't have a lead on Al Dalton.

Something was nagging at Carlyn. Her mind went to Leigh. In the weeks before her death, Leigh had also had a pretty bizarre run of bad luck. She was supposed to audition for the orchestra and her flute was stolen. Then her murderer had gone after Jamie. And now Ben was dead.

That's three of my old friends, Carlyn thought with a shiver. Three of the Five.

Jamie had been at Ben's funeral—but Brooke Tremont hadn't. She's in danger, Carlyn thought. All three of us are. But Brooke has no idea.

Carlyn picked up the phone and punched in Brooke's number at Kalamazoo State University.

Brooke picked it up on the second ring. "Carlyn!" she said over a blur of voices in the background. "Where are you calling from?"

"My room—why?"

"I thought you might still be in Middletown. How was Ben's funeral? I'm sorry I couldn't be there."

"It was awful. How are you?"

Actually, she could tell that everything was fine with Brooke. Better than fine. From the background noise, it sounded like there was a crowd partying in the suite Brooke shared with her roommates. "What's going on over there?" she asked.

"There's a party going on. Sorry. Our suite is, like, a total madhouse."

"Listen, Brooke," Carlyn broke in. "I've got something important to tell you—"

"Maybe I should call you back later," Brooke said absently. It's as if she didn't hear what I said, Carlyn thought in annoyance. "It's total chaos here. Oh, and speaking of chaos . . . guess who's getting married? Danielle Stevens."

Danielle was another one of their good friends from Middletown. During senior year, she, Brooke, and Carlyn had spent hours hanging out together, mostly in the mansion that Brooke called home.

"Danielle? That's great. I'm really happy for her and Brad."

"That's the amazing part," Brooke burst out. "She's not marrying Brad! She met another guy. Can you believe it? I hear Brad's taking it really hard."

"He always was a pretty jealous guy," Carlyn said. "Listen, Brooke, I hate to change the subject—"

"Carlyn, you forgot to ask me the most important question!" Brooke said.

Carlyn sighed impatiently. "What's that?"

"Who Danielle will choose for bridesmaids. You and I are definitely in. And I'll make sure she picks Jamie and—"

Carlyn held her breath, knowing what Brooke had almost said: "Leigh." The name hung between them like a bomb about to go off.

"Brooke," Carlyn said carefully, "do you ever think about Leigh?"

"I try not to," Brooke said in what for her was an unusually serious tone. "I mean, what happened to her was awful, but there's nothing any of us can do about it."

"I know," Carlyn said, "but now Ben is dead, too. It seems like too much of a coincidence. Leigh and Ben are dead, and Leigh's killer attacked Jamie. That's three of the Five, Brooke. You and I could be next."

"Me?" Brooke said in disbelief. It was clear the idea had never occurred to her.

"Yes, you," Carlyn said. "Whoever killed Leigh and attacked Jamie must be someone we all knew in Middletown. Otherwise, why would the attacker go for Leigh and then Jamie? And maybe he killed Ben, too."

"I thought Ben's death was an accident," said Brooke.

"That's what the police say."

"Listen," said Brooke, "I'm not trying to cut you off or anything, but you're starting to sound a little paranoid, Carlyn. Ben tried to lift more weight than he could handle—that sounds just like him to me. Leigh is gone and Jamie is going to be fine. And I've got to get ready for a dance. Life goes on."

Carlyn took a deep breath. Brooke had always been self-centered, and they'd always joked about it. Somehow it just wasn't very funny right now.

"I'll let you go," Carlyn said.

They said good-bye and hung up. I was only trying to help her, Carlyn thought. But maybe she's right. Could I be making too much of all this?

About twenty miles from the Indiana Tech campus, Bobby pulled his car off the highway and found a motel. That night, he dyed his hair blond—including his eyebrows and newly grown mustache.

When he got to the college, he headed straight for the campus store and bought himself some school sweatshirts and T-shirts. He also picked up a copy of the campus paper. Then he sat in his car circling ads for apartments.

He worked fast. Within three days, he had gotten himself a new studio apartment and a fake student ID. He'd also picked out a number of classes to attend. But most important, he'd put a bug on Carlyn's phone, using the equipment he had left over from his old Madison security job.

On Monday morning Bobby was sitting in Psych 101, listening to white-haired Professor Roger Barnard lecture his freshman class.

"Stimulus and response," said Barnard, writing the words in large letters on the blackboard that lined the base of the vast lecture hall. "If you learn nothing else from this next month of our work together, I want you to understand that all animal behavior—and some would say, all human behavior as well—is ruled by these two words."

In the third row of the large hall, Carlyn Alexander underlined the words in her notebook. Two seats behind her, Bobby watched her, then wrote them in his own notebook. He was wearing a dark blue Indiana Tech sweatshirt that made his blond hair look even lighter. Carlyn still had the same mop of reddish-brown hair that she'd had as a kid. He'd recognize her anywhere.

Professor Barnard droned on, something about assigning new lab partners for the next series of experiments. Bobby wasn't listening anymore. He watched Carlyn for a while, concentrating on the nape of her neck as she bent over her notebook. Then he started doodling in his notebook. "Scared to death," he wrote. He wrote it over and over and over again.

At just after two on Sunday morning Carlyn walked down the hall of her dorm and knocked on Sara Finney's door to see if she was still awake.

"Oh, sorry, I woke you up, didn't I?" Carlyn apologized as soon as Sara opened the door. Sara covered her eyes with her hands as she emerged, groaning, from the dark room.

"It's okay, come on in. I was only having the best dream of my life. Professor Baldwin and I were getting married!"

Carlyn laughed out loud. "I don't know, Sara. I think I just saved you from making the mistake of your life. Baldwin's sort of cute, but he's kind of stuffy, don't you think?"

"Oh, please," Sara said, turning on the light. "Like you've never had a thing for a teacher." She handed Carlyn an open bag of jelly beans.

"Speaking of getting married, my friend Danielle's wedding is coming up and I'm going to be a bridesmaid. It's going to be very traditional. Can you imagine me in a long pink taffeta dress?"

Sara giggled. "Not with hair your color red. I had to be a pink bridesmaid for my cousin, but at least my hair didn't clash with the outfit."

Carlyn groaned. "I've never been much of a fashion statement, so I don't really care about that. But I am sort of bummed about the money. The whole thing is going to cost a fortune. I mean, I'll have this dress I can never wear again, and I'm going to have to buy those awful dyed shoes—"

Sara threw open her closet and produced a pair of pink silk pumps. "I brought them with me to school. I figured it couldn't hurt to have an extra pair of party shoes, just in case. Why don't you borrow them for your wedding? Try them on."

Carlyn stepped into the shoes and stared at herself in Sara's mirror. She looked pretty silly wearing pink high heels with her long nightgown. The shoes were a bit tight, but she could deal with it for one day if it meant saving money. "I really appreciate this. Thank—"

The room was suddenly plunged into darkness. Sara shrieked and grabbed Carlyn's arm in a panicked grip.

"It's okay," Carlyn said, gently prying Sara's fingers from her arm. "It's just a power outage. Let's find the door and go find someone with a flashlight."

"Oh great, Val." Renee's voice floated down the hall through the darkness. "I told you that hot plate was going to overload the circuits."

"You also told me to make you coffee," Valerie replied indignantly.

"Why couldn't you just go down to the end of the hall and use the kitchen like everyone else?" Renee demanded.

"They're at it again," Sara said, sounding amused. "Even in the middle of a blackout Renee and Val can find something to argue about."

Shouting from several nearby rooms added to

85

the chaos. "Turn the lights on or I'm going to flunk!" a girl named Colleen yelled.

Carlyn heard the sound of someone—probably Val or Renee—fumbling in a drawer. Seconds later Carlyn saw Renee standing in her doorway, peering out into the hall, a flashlight in her hand.

"Great," Colleen said. "There goes my excuse. Now I have to study by flashlight."

"Will someone please call maintenance?" shouted another voice. "The whole dorm is out."

Carlyn moved toward her room and stopped, her heart pounding, as someone grabbed her from behind. Whoever it was, was even more scared than Carlyn was. She let out a scream that Carlyn recognized at once. "Molly, it's me, Carlyn," she said soothingly. Molly was definitely the most hysterical person on their floor.

"Thank goodness," Molly said. "I thought you might be a mugger."

"I just called campus security," Colleen reported. "They said they'll send someone over to look at the basement fuses."

"When?" Sara demanded.

"They said they'd be here soon," Colleen answered, "which means they should be here in about three hours."

Molly screamed again.

"Will you stop that already?" Carlyn snapped. She looked at Renee. "Could I could borrow that flash for a few minutes?"

Renee handed her the light. "Go right ahead."

"Where are you going?" Molly asked fearfully.

"Down to the basement," Carlyn said matter-of-factly as she headed for the stairwell. Then she made her voice sound all creepy. "Down where the monsters live."

Since the elevators were out the second- and first-floor stairwells were crowded with freshmen girls laughing and joking as they ran between floors, visiting each other in the dark.

Carlyn worked her way through the crowd until she reached the flight of stairs that led to the basement two stories below. She opened the door to the basement and stopped as a blast of cool, damp air hit her. This flight of stairs had a different feel to it. This was the original foundation of the building, and the old plaster walls smelled faintly of decay.

She began the descent, listening to the voices of the girls above her grow fainter. Except for the narrow beam of her light it was completely dark down here. And creepy.

Don't even think that way, Carlyn told herself sternly. She'd never been the hysterical type, like Molly, and she wasn't about to start now.

This is not a big deal, she thought. All you're going to do is find a fuse box.

Beneath her, one foot slipped a little on the damp stairs. Of course, she *would* have to do this in pumps, but she didn't dare take them off. What if she stepped on a nail or something? Impatiently, she used her free hand to gather her nightgown above her ankles. The movement threw her off balance.

Carlyn screamed as her feet suddenly went out from under her. In an instant she felt one pink satin pump fall off and the flashlight fly from her hand. The next thing she knew she was falling through the darkness.

# CHAPTER 17

Carlyn landed hard. For a long moment she couldn't catch her breath, and she realized she'd just found out what it meant to have the wind knocked out of her. When she could breathe again she realized that everything hurt—and warm, sticky blood was running down her forehead and her left leg.

Bit by bit Carlyn began to move her arms and legs. Nothing was broken, she decided, though everything seemed to be bruised. It would help if she had a light, but the flashlight had gone off when it fell, and she had no idea where it was.

She managed to sit up without too much pain, and then, holding onto either wall, she stood. That was a mistake. She'd done something to her left ankle, and it wouldn't support her weight. She sat back down on the stairs, wondering what to do next.

Instead of retracing her steps, Carlyn decided to go ahead and find the fuse box in the basement. She couldn't take too much more of this blackness.

Using the wall for support, she hobbled down the staircase. She stopped as her bare foot touched something covered with cloth. She bent down, reached out a groping hand, and realized it was her missing shoe—covered with something sticky, probably her own blood.

Carlyn dropped the shoe and reached the bottom of the stairs. She pushed her way through the door that led to the basement. She hadn't been down here since the beginning of the year when she'd stored her foot locker down here. She knew the cavernous room was filled with trunks, boxes, and suitcases.

Where would the fuse box be? Where most fuse boxes were—on the wall. With her hands straight out in front of her, Carlyn began to feel her way around the perimeter of the room.

"Bingo," she said aloud as her hands closed around a metal box.

If she'd had the flashlight, she might have seen the pair of scuffed shoes that were sticking out just to the side of the fuse box. If she hadn't been distracted by the pain in her ankle, she might have been aware that she wasn't alone. A tall, powerfully built figure stood just inches from her in the darkness.

. . .

Bobby held his breath as Carlyn came closer and closer. He'd always had good night vision. Although he couldn't make out her expression, he saw that she was opening the fuse box. He ducked behind a large packing carton as she threw the switches, and the lights came back on.

He'd come down to the basement to check out the phone wiring, but he'd tripped the light switches by accident. Before he could turn them back on, he'd heard the screams upstairs and he'd enjoyed the sound too much to put a stop to it. And surprise, surprise, his favorite girl in the dorm had come tumbling down the stairs. How convenient.

He could see her face now—her gray eyes rimmed with exhaustion and pain, her pretty nightgown stained with blood. Carlyn was not having a good night. And yet, Bobby realized, there was no fear in her, only a commonsense sort of relief from having found the fuse box.

Well, how about that, he thought with a reluctant twinge of admiration. This one could be a little tougher than Leigh or Ben. Leigh was a softie, a scaredy-cat. Ben was such a golden boy and under so much pressure to achieve that he only needed a little push. But Carlyn—

Carlyn turned and began limping toward the stairs. Bobby fought the temptation to reach out and grab her. It would be so easy. He had her down here, alone and injured.

Not yet, he decided. He was going to have too much fun playing this one out. There'd be plenty of time to scare her—to terrify her through and through. In fact he was going to take special delight in discovering what it was that would scare Carlyn Alexander beyond her worst nightmare.

The psych department's labs were housed in the natural sciences building, an old, hulking, ivy-covered monstrosity at the far corner of the quad. Carlyn arrived promptly, at five of three, but D. J. Thomas, her new lab partner, was already waiting for her on the building's front steps. The short, frizzy-haired girl was carrying a pile of books. With her free hand, she kept checking her watch as Carlyn approached.

"There you are," D.J. said with a relieved grin.

"We're supposed to be here at three, aren't we?" Carlyn asked her, as they headed inside. Her ankle was still sore from being scraped and sprained the other night, and she was proud of herself for getting across campus on time despite a slight limp.

"I know. I'm sorry," D.J. said. "It's just I take these things very seriously. I can't stand being late for appointments."

I guess not, thought Carlyn. This girl was wired. But on the other hand, D.J. had a reputation as a computer whiz and one of the smartest students in the freshman class. Carlyn knew she should be glad to have her for a partner. They made their way through the crowded lobby and started up the first flight of stone stairs.

"Well, you don't have to worry about me,"

Carlyn told her. "I'm very responsible. But I've got to tell you, I'm dreading this whole next week."

"Why?"

"Rats," Carlyn said with a shudder. "I can't stand rats." She wasn't even sure why she had such a phobia; all she knew was that just looking at the rodents was enough to make her shake.

D.J. looked surprised. "They're little white lab rats. They're harmless."

"Please," Carlyn said, holding up a hand. "Don't even talk about them."

D.J. giggled. "I guess you don't have a cat like I do."

"Why?"

"Buttons is always catching mice and bringing them home as presents."

"D.J.! Please!"

"Sorry. But, I mean, aren't you a psych major? You're going to have to work with rats a lot, you know."

"I've got a solution," Carlyn said, as they reached the third floor. "I'm going to change majors."

"Come on," said D.J. "Seriously."

"Well, what I was thinking, so that I could sort of ease my way into it . . . what would you say, if I do all the notes and write up all the reports, and this time around you do all the rat handling and feeding?"

"You're kidding," D.J. said, stopping short. Carlyn waited for her partner to get mad or something. But D.J. was beaming. "I hate writing up the reports." She held out her hand. "Carlyn," she said, "this is the beginning of a great lab partnership."

They shook on it and laughed.

The third floor hallways of the natural sciences building were narrow, twisting, and only dimly lit. Carlyn looked at the numbers on the doors. "How are we supposed to find this place? It's like a maze."

"This way," D.J. said, turning confidently to the right. Carlyn gave her a surprised look. "When I first got here," D.J. explained, "I came up to check if you were already here."

"When did you get here?" asked Carlyn. "At noon?"

D.J. blushed as she led the way into Lab 304. "What can I tell you?" she said. "You're scared of rats, I'm scared of being late."

All at once, Carlyn smelled the rodents. Then she heard them scurrying. More students were coming in the door behind her, or she might have turned and run.

The walls of the large lab were lined with rat cages. Students were milling around, looking in the cages as casually as if this were a pet shop filled with adorable puppies.

Susan Muller, the T.A. for their section, strode in wearing a lab coat and carrying a clipboard. "Everyone's here for Susan Muller's section of Barnard's Psych 101, right?" she asked.

I wish I weren't, Carlyn answered silently.

"Okay," Susan went on cheerfully. "Each team

needs to pick out an empty cage over there in the back and make a nice home for your rat. You'll find water bottles back there as well as a bag of wood shavings. Then when you're ready, come over here"—she pointed to a huge glass case loaded with rats, squirming and crawling on top of each other—"and pick out your subject."

"I think I'm going to throw up," Carlyn muttered.

"Don't worry," D.J. told her. "I'll handle this."

What's wrong with you? Carlyn asked herself. She had always been so levelheaded. What was there about those tiny creatures that made her flesh crawl?

Carlyn moved to the nearest open window. She was in the back of the building, facing the tree-lined street that ran alongside the campus. At least over here she could catch a breath of fresh, spring air, instead of that awful rodent smell.

D.J. was picking out their rat now. Carlyn tried not to look. But she peeked anyway and she saw D.J. rolling up her sleeve.

Carlyn turned away, sharply. And saw a rat dangling right in her face.

"What do you think?" asked Stu Howser, who was holding the red-eyed creature by the scruff of its neck. "Did I make a good choice?"

Carlyn didn't scream. But she did step back so quickly that she knocked into a pile of empty cages. One cage fell with a loud, clattering crash.

"Careful back there," she heard Susan Muller call.

"Thanks a lot," Carlyn snapped at Stu, who looked like he was trying not to laugh.

"Sorry," he said. "I figured us psych majors all have to get used to these little things. Here, want to hold him?"

Every muscle in Carlyn's body stiffened as Stu casually dropped his rat onto her shoulder. Then, in front of her entire psych lab, before she could stop herself, Carlyn let out an ear-piercing scream.

Bobby picked his own rat out of the cage, and turned around in time to watch Carlyn scream her head off.

Perfect, he thought, with a rush of satisfaction. Now he knew exactly how to get to her. He stroked the rat he'd taken from the cage. It was going to be very, very easy.

You're in luck, Carlyn, he thought as he watched Susan Muller remove the rat from Carlyn's shoulder. See, I used to be scared of rats, too, especially that day in the Whitlock house when I had one breathing in my face. But I got over my fear. Too bad you weren't so lucky.

He slipped out of the lab and into the crowded hallway. He was grinning so broadly that several students gave him strange looks.

He had it! He had the way to get Carlyn.

The plan was still a little vague, but he could feel it starting to take shape. It was like a picture when it started to develop. He kept seeing more of the details. It was all coming together. It was going to be absolutely perfect.

He burst through the building's double doors and out into the sunshine. Get ready, Carlyn, he thought. You and I are going to be running a little rat experiment of our own.

# CHAPTER 18

" T his is so great that you have a machine that doesn't cut you off," D.J. said, "so I can just read you all my notes like this." She gave a little giggle.

Bobby giggled, too, imitating her laugh. He was lying on his back on his bed, his hands behind his head, listening to the message being recorded on Carlyn's answering machine. "Yeah, D.J.," he said aloud. "It is lucky."

D.J. was still talking. "Let's see . . . what else. Oh, yeah, one other thing. I think we should mention that the rat can probably hear the other bells being rung in other cages, which could skew our data, because that means our rat is hearing bells sometimes and then not getting fed. That's all for now. If you could type this up, like we agreed, that

98

would be great." There was a pause, then she went on, "Listen, I'm assuming you got my last two very long messages and that you've already typed up those notes as well. I know I'm a pain, but would you please, please, please call me back to confirm this? I worry, as you know. Also, I want to see a copy, for my files." D.J. added a singsong "Bye" and then hung up.

Bobby counted to ten, then dialed Carlyn's number.

"Hi, this is Carlyn," the machine began. "I'm not in right now, but—"

"But that means that I can mess you up totally," said Bobby. He pushed the * key on his phone. Carlyn's machine beeped. Then he punched in the authorization code printed under the lid of her answering machine, which he'd checked when he bugged her phone. The machine beeped again, then beeped one more time to indicate that it had recorded one message. The tape rewound, then played back D.J.'s message. When it was done it beeped three times. Bobby checked the little instruction card he had taped to his wall. "Rewind and erase," he read. "When you don't need to hear messages anymore." He pressed 3.

Later that day, humming happily, he went to his room and booted up his rented computer terminal. Using a modem, Bobby logged into the campus system. He entered D.J.'s password. A flashing message appeared on his screen.

"D.J. CARLYN HERE. I THOUGHT YOU WERE GOING TO GET ME YOUR LAB NOTES

DAY BY DAY SO I COULD KEEP TYPING THEM UP. IT'S WEDNESDAY AFTERNOON AND I STILL HAVEN'T HEARD FROM YOU. WHAT'S THE STORY?"

"Bye-bye," said Bobby. He hit Clear Screen, and the message disappeared.

Carlyn scanned the crowded lecture hall. It certainly wasn't like D.J. to be late, but she was. Maybe she's been sick, Carlyn thought.

It was Friday morning and psych lecture was about to begin. Professor Barnard was writing some notes on the board. Carlyn turned and watched the rest of the class filing in. She couldn't understand it. She hadn't heard from D.J. once all week. What did she do? Do the report herself, and leave Carlyn out of it altogether? Was there something wrong with D.J. or was this some kind of trick to make Carlyn look bad? She knew D.J. had a reputation for being competitive, but this was ridiculous.

"Carlyn!" D.J. had come up behind her.

"There you are," Carlyn said. "What's been going on, I—"

"I can't believe you!" D.J. snapped. "I thought you said you were really responsible!"

"I am," Carlyn said evenly. "But what about you? I've been—"

D.J. shook her head in disbelief and interrupted again. "What about me? All right, look, just give me the report so I can at least read it once for typos before class."

"What report?" Carlyn asked.

D.J. looked like she might have a stroke. "What report?" Her right eye was twitching. "Carlyn, are you trying to tell me that you don't have our report typed up?"

"D.J.," Carlyn said, "I've been putting computer mail messages on your terminal all week. I slipped notes under your door, I called—"

"You are such a total liar!" D.J. sputtered. Heads were starting to turn. "I left you the notes on your answering machine, but you never called me back. Not once."

"That's impossible," Carlyn said, turning red. "I didn't get a single message."

Susan Muller, the T.A., was walking up the aisle now, collecting lab reports. Professor Barnard stepped up to the mike on the podium. "Please hand in those lab reports, I'd like to begin."

"Now what do we do?" D.J. demanded. "You don't expect me to take the rap for this, do you?"

"D.J.," Carlyn said, "I really don't know what to say. I—"

"Reports?" Susan Muller was standing in front of them, holding a pile of reports—the reports that everyone except Carlyn and D.J. had completed.

"We seem to be having a little confusion here," Carlyn told Susan, trying to smile.

"I need a new partner," D.J. said quickly.

"What?" Carlyn gasped.

"Carlyn was supposed to type up our report but she didn't," D.J. hurried on. "She didn't return a single one of my calls. I mean, this is what I don't

101

like about the whole lab partner setup. Your partner can completely mess you up."

Carlyn felt herself turn beet red as D.J.'s voice rose. Once again the entire class was staring at her.

"Is there a problem?" boomed Professor Barnard's deep voice from the front of the lecture hall.

"They don't have their report," Susan Muller called back.

"It's her fault," D.J. said loudly, pointing her finger at Carlyn. There were snickers from the rest of the students. Carlyn prayed that the floor would open up beneath her feet and swallow her.

"See me after class," Professor Barnard said, obviously annoyed. "I can't hold up this lecture any longer."

Carlyn and D.J. ended up sitting right next to each other. They both stared straight ahead. "Thanks a lot," Carlyn whispered.

"Don't blame me," D.J. growled back. "Blame yourself."

Carlyn tried to take careful notes during the lecture, but it was hard to concentrate. She kept turning the thing over in her mind. Her answering machine was pretty new. She'd never had a problem with it before. Carlyn couldn't believe that it had malfunctioned like that. And what about the messages she'd left on the computer net and the notes she'd slipped under D.J.'s door?

Was D.J. deliberately sabotaging her? And if she was, why? Either D.J. was crazy or— At the moment Carlyn couldn't think of any other possibility.

After the lecture D.J. strode up to the podium, and Carlyn followed. Professor Barnard was gathering his notes. "Ah yes," he said, looking down at them from under shaggy white brows. "The two delinquents."

He listened briefly to both sides of the argument. "Well," he said frowning, "it doesn't take a psychology professor to conclude that one of you is lying."

"It's her," D.J. put in. Carlyn glared at her.

"But," continued Barnard, "no matter which one of you is lying . . . I must say that I'm disappointed in you, Carlyn. You shouldn't have made an agreement like this in the first place. There is no substitute for going to the lab and getting your hands dirty."

"That was a mistake, I agree," Carlyn said, trying to keep her voice steady. "But as far as the report—"

"As far as the rest of it goes," continued Barnard, "all I can really do is have you both redo the experiment."

"I won't work with her again," D.J. said, folding her arms in front of her chest.

Professor Barnard frowned. "In that case, you'll both have to do the experiment separately." With that he turned away to answer questions from other students.

"I don't know what your problem is," Carlyn said as she followed D.J. up the aisle.

D.J. turned around sharply. "You're my problem. *Were* my problem." D.J. continued to walk

103

ahead of her, pushing her way through the double doors.

Outside, the bright sunshine and warm breeze seemed totally out of place to Carlyn. Only a thunderstorm could have matched her mood. She thought of what her mother would say: When you're angry at someone, try to look at the situation from the other person's point of view.

Okay, she'd try to look at the thing from D.J.'s side. Maybe D.J. was just overloaded with work this week and couldn't get to the experiment. So she panicked and decided to lay the blame on Carlyn.

In any case, it should be easy for me to put something like this in perspective, Carlyn thought. Missing a lab paper was no big deal.

Her thoughts were interrupted by shouts from Sara Finney and Colleen Morgan.

"Are you okay? We heard about the big scene in psych class," Sara said as they walked toward her.

"Which one?" Carlyn asked grimly. "The rat scene in lab or today's little drama?"

"Today's," Colleen answered.

"Great," Carlyn said. "It hasn't even been a half hour, and already I'm the campus joke."

"Everyone's saying it was D.J.'s fault," Colleen assured her.

"That girl's so intense, she probably blew a fuse," Sara added loyally.

Carlyn shrugged. "I really don't understand what's going on with her. But the worst part is now

I have to do the rat experiment by myself. I guess that's what comes of trying to get out of something. Now it's going to be just me and the rats."

"Don't worry," Sara assured her. "Colleen will go with you."

"Are you crazy?" Colleen said. "Even flies terrify me."

"All right. All three of us will go," Sara said. She draped her arm around Carlyn's shoulder. "Okay?"

"Okay," Carlyn said. She smiled for the first time since class. "Thanks."

By lunchtime Carlyn was starving. And after the incident with D.J., she needed the comfort of food. Preferably food with lots of chocolate in it. She walked into the cafeteria, planning to treat herself to double portions of everything, especially ice cream. As she passed her ID through the security system the machine buzzed loudly.

"Hold on there," the security woman told her.

Ahead of her two guys turned around. "Uh-oh!" one of them cracked. "Student impostor."

"Step aside, please," the guard told her gruffly.

Rolling her eyes, Carlyn moved out of the way of the students filing in behind her. This obviously wasn't going to be her day.

The security guard was studying Carlyn's card. She ran it through the machine several times. Each time, the machine buzzed. "Your card is invalid," she finally said.

"Well that's impossible," Carlyn said. "I mean, I go to this college. I eat here every day."

"Not today you don't."

Carlyn stared at the guard in disbelief. "What am I supposed to do?"

"Go to the security office, see if you can straighten it out. Have your parents paid your tuition?"

That did it. Carlyn took the card back. "Thank you," she said as politely as she could manage. "I'll be back."

"You'd better come back with a different card," the guard told her.

The campus security office was on the ground floor of Dana Hall, on the south end of the main quad. Carlyn's stomach started to rumble as she walked across campus.

She passed the main gate and stopped. Just two blocks away, off campus, was a health food restaurant called the Kitchen. The Kitchen's cheap and delicious veggieburgers and desserts had made it a popular student hangout for years. Dealing with security could take a while, Carlyn knew. They were famous for their red tape. She might as well get some food first. She turned the knob and pushed out through the heavy wrought-iron gate.

Later, when she returned to campus, she was feeling more cheerful. She reached the heavy wrought-iron gate and saw that it was locked. No problem. She reached for her ID.

That was when it hit her.

"Oh, no!" she muttered. She ran her card through the magnetic strip and hoped the gate would click open. Nothing happened. "Great!" She banged her hand against the gate in frustration.

She picked up the yellow campus phone and called security. It took them twenty minutes to send a guard to the gate. It took another ten minutes for her to convince the guard to let her in. Then she waited on line for another twenty minutes at campus security's main office. Only to be told she would have to go to the registrar's office.

And now it was time for her modern art lecture. No, today was definitely not her day.

That night Carlyn sat in her room eating the leftovers Sara and Colleen had sneaked out of the cafeteria for her. "Thanks, guys," she said as she broke off a piece of corn bread.

"I'd rather feed you than feed that rat," Colleen said with a shudder.

Carlyn took a bite of chicken and waved her sheet of lab notes. "Well, thanks again for coming with me to the lab. I think I'll be able to handle it by myself the rest of the week."

"If you can't, just let us know," Sara said as she and Colleen headed out the door.

Wiping her hands on a tissue, Carlyn sat down at her computer terminal. She took another bite of her dinner. Never had cafeteria food tasted so delicious.

Sitting next to her computer was the note she had found slipped under her door tonight. "Thanks again for trying to mess up my grade. It'll

107

be interesting to see who does better this week.—
D.J."

Unbelievable. She crumpled the note into a ball
and slipped it into her pocket. Later she'd show it
to Sara and Colleen.

Okay, Carlyn, she told herself. Let's rock and
roll. She wanted an A on this report, both because
she was naturally competitive, and because she
didn't want D.J. to have the satisfaction of getting a
better grade.

Carlyn reached behind the terminal and hit the
On button. The main campus menu sprang into focus. ENTER YOUR PERSONAL PASSWORD, was
the flashing message.

PHYLLIS, typed Carlyn. It was her middle
name. She hated it so much that she had never told
it to anyone. So she figured it was safe as a password. She hit return.

PASSWORD INVALID. PLEASE TRY AGAIN.

Okay, stay calm, Carlyn ordered herself. She
had obviously hit the keys wrong.

PHYLLIS, she typed again, typing slowly this
time and watching each of the keys as she hit
them.

PASSWORD INVALID. PLEASE TRY AGAIN.

She did try again. And again. Then she
punched the keyboard with her fist.

PASSWORD INVALID. PLEASE TRY AGAIN.

"That wasn't my password, you stupid machine," Carlyn told the terminal. "That was me
punching you."

She stood up quickly, forgetting that she had

her dinner plate resting on her lap. The food landed facedown with a splat. "Terrific," she said aloud. "What else can possibly go wrong today?"

Trying to stay calm, she flipped through the pages of her pink campus phone directory, found the number she wanted, and dialed it. It rang about fifteen times. Carlyn pressed the phone hard against her ear, willing someone to answer, and refusing to hang up.

"Computer center," said a woman's voice. "Can I help you?"

"Uh, well, I'm a freshman over in Binghampton Hall, and I'm trying to use my computer and I keep getting password invalid—"

"Are you typing it in correctly?" The woman sounded as if she had heard this complaint about six hundred times today already.

"Yes, I'm sure I am. I've tried it again and again."

"Name?"

"Carlyn Alexander. I had a problem with my regular ID today as well. I don't know if those two things could be related . . ."

"I'm checking."

"I went to campus security but they said to go to the registrar and by the time I got there it was closed, and in the meantime, I can't eat, so—"

"I said I was checking." The systems operator was sounding more irritated by the minute.

Carlyn looked at the plate of food on the floor and winced. Why was her entire life such a mess all of a sudden?

"Carlyn?" the woman on the phone asked. She sounded very surprised. "You're Carlyn P. Alexander?"

"That's right."

The woman whistled.

"What is it?" Carlyn asked. She was starting to feel very uneasy.

"Carlyn," the woman said, "according to our computer records, you're deceased."

# CHAPTER 19

arlyn felt her spine prickle. "I'm deceased?" she asked weakly.

"That's what my records say."

Carlyn laughed, but her laugh sounded crazy to her. "It's got to be a mistake. I'm not dead. It's just—"

"These things happen," the systems operator said. "But you'll have to come into the office tomorrow. We'll need some proof that you're actually you and not someone playing a prank. We need proof that Carlyn Alexander is actually alive. If this is a mistake, we can have it corrected within twenty-four hours."

"Twenty-four hours! But I've got work to do."

"I understand that. I've got work to do, too."

"What am I supposed to do in the meantime?"

Carlyn asked, trying to keep the panic out of her voice.

"You can use the terminals at the library. Ask the reference desk for the password."

"But I'll need to show a valid ID."

"Then go to the registrar."

"Oh, great."

"Come by the computer center in the morning," the woman advised. "Ask to speak to the supervisor and be sure to bring some valid identification."

"Thanks a lot," Carlyn said as the woman hung up.

Carlyn sat down on her window seat and stared out into the night. Somehow the school's computer system had entered her as deceased. How could this happen? What had the woman said —something about having to prove that she wasn't playing a prank? Maybe someone was playing one on her. That someone would have to both be computer adept—someone who could get into the system at high security levels—and someone who didn't like her very much.

Computers. It didn't take Carlyn long to come up with a name linked with computers. D.J.! She was supposed to be an ultra-hacker. But was she really that vindictive? Carlyn thought for a moment. There was no other explanation. The more she thought about it, the angrier she got. She picked up the phone again and punched in D.J.'s number.

"Hello?"

"The computer center says I'm listed as dead," Carlyn said.

There was a silence. "Who is this?" D.J. demanded.

"This is Carlyn. Congratulations, D.J. Your little trick worked."

"What little trick?"

"My student ID is suddenly invalid. I can't get into the cafeteria or even through the campus gates, and I can't log onto the computer net. You're successfully wrecking my life. Now please fix it so I can go back to work."

"I really don't know what you're talking about," D.J. said.

"D.J.," Carlyn said evenly. "Either you do your little computer trick again and reactivate my ID, or I'm going to the dean."

"I think you've gone insane," D.J. said.

"Look who's talking," Carlyn said. She couldn't help it. She was so mad, she felt like she was eight and back on the playground at recess.

"I'm totally serious," D.J. said. "I'm really getting worried about you. Have you thought about going over to Health Services and talking to one of the shrinks there? They're free for students, you know."

Carlyn couldn't keep from raising her voice. "I can't!" she shouted. "I don't have an ID! Remember?" Trying to regain control, she went on, "Please, D.J. Why are you doing this to me? Just tell me that. Are you afraid I'll beat you out for best in the class or something?"

113

"You're a total wacko," D.J. said calmly. Then she hung up.

Carlyn called back three minutes later. There was no answer. "I know you're there, D.J.," Carlyn muttered. "I just talked to you." After ten rings, she hung up. Fine, she told herself, pulling on a sweater. You won't answer the phone, I'll talk to you in person.

D.J. lived in Hamilton House, an older house directly across the quad that had been converted to a student co-op. Carlyn could see the room lights burning in the big ramshackle house.

Carlyn crossed the campus in half her usual time and took the rickety front stairs two at a time. Students in the co-ops were supposed to take responsibility for maintenance. Obviously the group in Hamilton House hadn't gotten it together. She rang the doorbell and waited.

Eventually the door was opened by a bearded guy in a striped bathrobe, who looked at Carlyn as if she belonged to some exotic species he'd never seen before.

"Is D.J. here?" Carlyn asked impatiently.

"Upstairs," he said, letting her in.

The door to D.J.'s room was ajar. But the light was off. For the first time since Carlyn had left her dorm, she slowed down. The room had a dead look.

"D.J." she called, walking toward the door.

No answer.

She put her hand on the door and pushed. It

114

swung inward. But there wasn't enough light from the hall for her to see much.

"D.J.?" She fumbled for the wall switch. The wall felt wet and sticky.

Then she found the switch and flicked on the light.

The wall, she saw, was smeared with blood.

Then she turned and looked into the room.

She nearly fainted.

# CHAPTER 20

arlyn doubled over and started to gag. She couldn't believe what she was seeing. Blood splattered the walls and floor.

Taking a deep breath, Carlyn forced herself to stand up. And then she realized that there was something pinned to the wall. At first she wasn't sure what it was. It was long and furry and . . .

A severed cat's tail was pinned to the wall with a knife.

As waves of nausea flooded her she realized that something else was pinned to the wall with the knife—a note.

In a haze, she moved closer so she could read it.

"A tail for a tattletale," the note read. "Thank

you so much for complaining about me to Professor Barnard." The note was signed Carlyn.

Carlyn felt dizzy. She wanted to run from this horror, but her body refused to move. This had to be a nightmare, she had to be dreaming. It couldn't possibly be real.

A bloodcurdling howl filled the hall. Carlyn jumped straight up, her heart hammering.

She whirled around. She didn't see anyone in the room.

Then she felt something brush against her leg.

It was Buttons. The cat was running in crazed circles, making an awful yowling sound. Most of her tail was gone. In its place was a bloody stump.

"Oh, you poor thing," Carlyn said. She knelt to try to catch the terrified animal and froze at the sound of an ear-shattering scream.

D.J. stood in the doorway, looking down at the cat. Her hands went to her face as she screamed over and over again.

Carlyn just stood there, unable to speak or move. When she held her hands out toward D.J., as if to comfort her, she saw that they were covered with blood.

"Come on in, Carlyn," said Dean Skelton stiffly. He stood up as Carlyn opened the door.

The dean's office was lined with dark walnut paneling. Two high-backed chairs sat on either side of a large oak desk. He gestured to the chair on the right. "Have a seat."

It wasn't until Carlyn sat down that she saw

D.J., sitting in the other seat. D.J.'s eyes were rimmed with red, and there were dark circles under her eyes. I had a bad night too, believe me, thought Carlyn. D.J. started to rise, as if to defend herself.

"It's okay, Donna Jo," the Dean said. "Please, both of you, sit."

Dean Skelton was an overweight man with a large, shiny bald head. Students made fun of the perpetual smile he wore as he walked around the campus. Well, that smile was finally gone.

"What I'd like to do—" the dean began.

"My parents are going to sue you, Carlyn," D.J. lashed out. "You're going to be paying vet bills for the rest of your life, and—"

Dean Skelton held up a large hand. "Hold on, D.J."

"I'm sorry," D.J. said. She was shaking. "I just can't believe anyone is sick enough to do that to a cat."

"I didn't do it," Carlyn said. "You've got to believe me."

"Liar!"

"Quiet, both of you!" the dean said sharply. "I'm going to ask the questions here. Understood? Carlyn, why don't you start by explaining this?"

He held out the bloodstained tattletale note. There was a jagged hole in the center of the paper where the knife had been.

"Dean Skelton," Carlyn began, "this is all as confusing to me as it is to you."

"That's a lie!" hissed D.J. But the dean forced

her to be quiet. Carlyn looked at the dean the whole time she was talking. It wasn't until she had told the whole story that she finally glanced over at D.J. Somehow she wasn't prepared for the look of intense hatred on the other girl's face. "We already called the police," D.J. said, her lower lip trembling. She jabbed her finger at Carlyn. "They'll prove you're lying."

Dean Skelton cleared his throat. "Now listen to me, both of you," he ordered. "What happened last night is extremely serious. There's no room for that sort of cruelty on this campus. Whoever is responsible for torturing that animal will be asked to leave the school immediately."

Carlyn blinked back tears and reached into her pocket for a tissue. Instead her hand closed around something small and crumpled. Puzzled, she pulled out the paper and smoothed it out on her lap. It was the note from D.J.

She had forgotten all about the note, but she was suddenly incredibly glad she'd saved it. It would at least prove part of her story.

Suddenly, the tiny hairs on the back of her neck started to rise. She was looking at the two notes—the scrawling handwriting, the odd *t*'s and *l*'s. They matched perfectly!

"Oh, my God!" she said. "Look at this." Carlyn handed the dean the wrinkled bit of paper. "This is a note D.J. slipped under my door yesterday afternoon. Look at the two handwritings. They're identical. *She* wrote both notes."

She stared at D.J. in horror as she realized what

119

this proved. "But that means you tortured your own cat," she said in disbelief. "Why? Would you really go that far just to try to hurt me?"

Both the dean and D.J. studied the two notes. Then D.J. looked up, her eyes blazing. "Dean Skelton," she said, "this girl is truly dangerous." She grabbed the first note. "I never wrote this! I never slipped any note under her door! This isn't even my handwriting. Look!"

She started writing on Dean Skelton's desk blotter, but he took her hand and stopped her. "D.J.," he said firmly, "sit down!" The dean paused, pushing his glasses up on the bridge of his nose. "Now I'm only going to say this once. The police are investigating this matter, and I'll abide by their judgment in the case. But in the meantime, while I'm waiting for that police report, I want this feud between the two of you dropped. It goes no further. Understood?" He looked at each of them in turn, and Carlyn could tell that he was furious. "Furthermore, you can each consider yourself on probation until this matter is resolved. If I have any more trouble from either one of you, I suggest you begin looking for another school."

Bobby lay on his bed, roaring with laughter. He was listening to the tapes he had made of Carlyn's latest phone calls. He replayed one of his favorites, her argument with D.J., three or four times, laughing harder each time. Her call to her mother in which she nervously told her about her meeting with the dean was also pretty hilarious. But what amused him most was that Carlyn was the only person smart enough to see the link between Leigh's and Ben's death. Carlyn was the only one who knew that the Five were all in danger. But Carlyn had no idea at all that she was already caught in his trap.

The lamps that lit the paths of the quadrangle were already on. Dusk had fallen. Straight ahead loomed the large brick face of the old sciences building. Carlyn walked slowly.

It was after seven that same evening. Her rat was probably getting pretty hungry; she was an hour late. But still, Carlyn was in no rush. Just the thought of those dark, deserted, twisting hallways made her shudder. And what would be her prize for finding her way through that maze? Lab 304, a room filled with rats.

She passed a post with a gray metal box—a campus phone. She could call Sara and Colleen and ask them to chaperon her one more time. But they were probably out. And even if they weren't, she would feel foolish. What had happened to old fearless Carlyn?

Plenty had happened, come to think of it. She tried unsuccessfully to blot out the image of the tailless cat, and looked up at the building again. There were only one or two lights in the whole place, and none that she could see on the third floor. She mounted the steps. She had a crazy nightmare image of a huge white rat, the size of a linebacker, waiting behind the door with an ax.

121

Good thinking, Carlyn. That was really the way to calm herself down. She tried to focus on something else. Her dream had always been to continue on after college and go to psych grad school. If she didn't get expelled for torturing D.J.'s cat, then that dream was still alive. Sooner or later, she would have to get over this phobia. It might as well be now.

She passed the second-floor stairwell, turned up the next staircase, and walked right into a tall, powerfully built man, holding a long, wooden stick.

"Where are you going?" he demanded.

"I—I—I—"

Carlyn blinked as she realized she was facing the custodian.

"There's no one up there," he said as she headed past him. "And I'm leaving."

Just her luck, thought Carlyn. Tonight no one else was working late. She was going to be alone with the rats.

"I'll only be a few minutes," Carlyn called back. She wondered if he could hear her heart pounding.

As she walked through the dimly lit hallway, she had an even worse thought. What if she *wasn't* alone? As if her fear had prompted it, she immediately got the distinct feeling that there was indeed someone behind her. Someone following her. She whirled.

She stared down the dark lab-lined hallway. She was sure that something had moved just out of sight just as she turned. No. Her mind was playing tricks on her. Still, she had the eerie feeling that if she walked back down that hallway—just around that corner, someone was waiting.

Sure. Another giant rat with an ax. She forced herself to keep going. When she got to the lab, she turned on all the lights. She made as much noise as she could. She tried not to look at the rows of rat cages. Just focus in on the one disgusting beast you're in charge of, she told herself.

The moment she rang the little bell, the rat in her cage started racing around frantically, staring up at her with those beady red eyes. Well, the experiment was working, anyway.

She opened the glass top of the cage, dropped in some food pellets, and slammed the cage shut again. Yuck! She looked away as the rat eagerly gobbled up its dinner.

Watch! she told herself, it's part of the experiment. But she didn't look back at the cage. Instead she kept her eyes firmly glued to—

What was she looking at?

It took her a moment to realize.

Next to her rat's cage was another cage. And next to that was a black-and-white composition notebook. And written in a small careful handwriting on the cover were the words D. J. Thomas. It was D.J.'s lab report.

She could hear her rat scrabbling around in its cage, looking for more pellets. But she was no longer listening. She moved toward the notebook.

Something about that handwriting pulled her forward.

Then she realized what it was. The note—the note she had gotten from D.J.

She pulled it out of her pocket and smoothed it on the large wooden lab table beside the notebook. Next she opened the notebook and began skimming the pages of the lab report. Then she looked back at the note, then back at D.J.'s lab report.

Suddenly, she looked up, gazing around the lab.

She was scared to death. The two handwritings didn't match.

Which meant that D.J. was telling the truth. And that meant that it wasn't D.J. who had been causing all the trouble. It was someone else—someone sick—someone dangerous—someone clever enough to make it all point to D.J.—but someone who was really after *her*. . . .

Suddenly she had an explanation for all the insanity, all the inexplicable things that had been happening to her and the rest of the Five. And the explanation scared her more deeply than anything that had happened so far. It all came down to one word—Bobby.

# CHAPTER 21

obby Wimmer. She remembered now. He was the one person who hated the Five. He killed Leigh and Ben—and now he was after her.

Carlyn took a step back, her body rigid with fear. She was alone in a building on the edge of campus. The buildings nearest to her were all administration buildings and all deserted at this hour. Leigh had been killed in a deserted campus building at night. And just like Leigh, Carlyn knew that if she screamed, no one would hear her.

She tried to stay calm and walk, but the minute she was out in the hallway she broke into a run. She ran past lab after lab, then stopped, trying to remember where the nearest stairwell was. She turned to her right, racing down another hallway that looked identical to the one she was in.

The door to the stairs was just ahead of her. She pushed it open and took so many stairs at a time that she was sure she was going to fall. The ankle that she'd sprained in the basement twinged with pain, but she ignored it, pushing herself to go faster.

Downstairs, she burst through the double doors that led outside. She didn't bother to see if the doors closed and locked behind her. Or if someone followed her out.

She raced across campus, running as hard as she could even though her lungs were aching and she could barely put weight on her ankle.

She fell twice as she ran up the stairs to her dorm room, but each time she scrambled back to her feet and kept going.

"Hey, Alexander, slow it down!" Sara called indignantly as Carlyn dashed past her.

Carlyn didn't turn to answer. She couldn't stop until she was safely back in her room. She found her key, pushed the door open, and slammed it shut behind her.

She fell onto her bed, gasping for breath, not even bothering to turn on the light. As soon as her breathing began to slow she rolled over, reaching out for the phone.

But as she rolled over, she felt something warm beneath her cheek. Something furry.

# CHAPTER 22

A rat!

Screaming, Carlyn jumped up. Nausea rose in her stomach.

"A rat!" she screamed. "A rat in my bed!"

She was shaking so hard, she felt as if her knees would give out. There was a rat in her bed. He'd gotten into her room and left a rat on her pillow.

She stood in the dark dorm room and screamed with every ounce of strength she had left. The sound ripped out of her as if it would never stop.

Her throat was raw but the terror kept pouring out. She couldn't stop even when she heard her friends pounding on her door.

"Carlyn, what's wrong?" That was Renee's voice. "Carlyn, open the door now!"

"Do you want us to call the police?" Valerie asked.

Finally, her friends' voices penetrated Carlyn's panic. She opened the door and nearly fell into Sara's arms.

"What's going on?" Sara asked. "What is it?"

Carlyn pointed helplessly at her bed.

Someone turned on the light, and someone else shrieked. "Oh, gross!" she heard one girl say. "There are rats in the building!"

Carlyn bit back another scream as the rat began to move, leaving a little smear of blood on her pillow. It moved very slowly, and soon she saw why. It was dragging both of its back legs, which were twisted at an odd angle.

"Oh my God," Carlyn said. "Someone broke its legs." Not "someone" she reminded herself, Bobby Wimmer. How could anyone be that warped?

Total chaos broke out. Girls were shouting, other girls kept sticking their head in the door and screaming. Carlyn made her way through the crowd toward the phone, stretching the cord as far as it would go—away from her bed.

"It stopped moving!" someone was yelling. Carlyn could see the rat, in the middle of her bed, panting. Its beady eyes seemed to be staring directly at her.

She called the police first, her fingers trembling so badly she had to dial three times. Then she called campus security. They said they would check out the Natural Sciences building before coming over to talk to her.

128

It was the exterminator who arrived first. Someone in the dorm must have called him. Out of the corner of her eye she saw the girls backing away from the bed to make room for him. He was a tall man with blond hair.

Letting him deal with the rat, Carlyn called D.J. next. "I know you don't believe anything I say anymore," Carlyn began. "But I just want you to know that there's a crazy psycho who's been playing a sick joke on both of us. And he probably has something a lot worse planned. So be careful because—"

"Who is this?" the voice asked.

Carlyn froze. The girl's voice didn't sound familiar. "D.J.?"

"No, this is Laura, one of her housemates. I think D.J.'s at the library. And then she said she had to go feed her rat."

"Tell her to call Carlyn. It's very, very important."

She stepped out of the way as the exterminator began to spray a clear liquid along the floorboards.

"Excuse me, miss?"

It was the exterminator. "Hi," he said, holding his hand out. "Brian Phillips." She didn't shake his hand. "I took that rat out of here and put some spray down."

"Great," Carlyn said. "Thanks."

"Listen," he said. "I saw some droppings. You should probably put out a few glue traps. We're giving them away free to customers these days. I have them down in the truck. You'll have to come down with me. I'm late for another job."

129

"Okay," Carlyn told him.

"This way," he said. "My truck is right over there."

She followed after him, wondering how in the world she was going to convince the police that they ought to be out looking for Bobby Wimmer. Where were the police anyway?

The exterminator's van was parked in the shadows behind the dorm. "Here we go," he said, opening the back door. He reached inside and pulled out some small black cardboard boxes. He held them out to her, his other hand in his pocket.

"Thanks," Carlyn said, starting forward. That was when she read the name on the man's uniform. "Glen."

"Glen?" she asked. The man looked blank. Then she remembered. He had said his name was Brian.

Glen was staring at her strangely. His deep-set brown eyes suddenly looked very familiar.

Carlyn took a step back, but he lunged forward, whipping his hand out of his pocket. Carlyn saw a blur of white handkerchief as Bobby clapped his hand over her mouth. Fear flooded through her and she screamed, but her screams were muffled by the handkerchief. Bobby was pressing it hard against her mouth. She smelled something strong and medicinal. Then he was dragging her back toward the van, pinning her against the doors. Carlyn was feeling weaker and weaker.

Bobby's eyes stared into hers. "Guess what, Carlyn," he said as she struggled uselessly. "You and I have a little date tonight. I've been planning it for years."

Carlyn was still struggling, but she could feel the strength draining out of her. And no matter how she twisted her head, he kept the handkerchief pressed over her nose and mouth.

Everything started to blur, and Bobby's voice faded away into the distance. "Carlyn," she heard him say. She could no longer see him clearly. "I can't tell you how great this feels. Congratulations, you're victim number three."

Then everything went black.

# CHAPTER 23

It felt as if someone were banging Carlyn's head with a hammer. And her mouth—her mouth was clogged, as if it were stuffed with cotton. I'm dead, Carlyn thought groggily. This is what it feels like to be dead.

Another bang on her head. She didn't really feel it fully, but the blow jolted her eyes open. She saw dark windows, a metal roof. Her head seemed to be resting on corrugated metal. Then her eyes closed again. She couldn't keep them open. She felt as if she were floating, drifting, through a dark inky sea. Until finally—

Something in her head told her she had come to a stop. She had landed. But where? She didn't want to open her eyes. She wanted to stay asleep.

She had a vague memory of something bad, of

danger. The danger wasn't in the sleep place, though; it was in the awake place. She kept her eyes shut.

But now she was becoming aware of something else. Physical sensations. She was cold. She was lying on something cold and hard. And there was a strange smell, a smell that made her hungry. Even stranger, she felt greasy. Still keeping her eyes closed, she lifted her hand to her face to touch her skin. But her hand didn't move.

She opened her eyes. She struggled to move her arms and legs, and realized they were tied with rope.

She rolled around like a beetle on its back. She was still groggy. But she was remembering now what had happened to her. And she was beginning to understand where she was.

She was lying on the cold cement floor . . . in the lab . . . and what was that smell? . . . peanut butter! She was covered with it. She could feel the greasy stuff all over her hair, her face, her neck, her stomach.

She heard footsteps approaching. Heard the sound of someone humming. "Scared to death . . . scared to death . . . Little Carlyn is scared to death."

Bobby walked into the room, carrying a red metal can of kerosene. He winked at her and started sloshing the kerosene all around the lab.

"You finally recognize me, huh?" he said. "A little late, though, right?"

She tried to speak, but her mouth was gagged. She made a helpless, gurgling sound.

"What's the matter?" Bobby asked politely. "I'm spilling the kerosene? Don't worry. You're probably going to be eaten by the rats way before the fire gets you."

Carlyn twisted in horror. The rats were scampering in their cages, already excited by the smell of peanut butter.

Bobby kept spreading the fuel. "Can you believe that D.J. would be crazy enough to do something like this?" he asked, shaking his head. "Me neither. But the cops will after I plant all the evidence in her room."

Bobby had finished pouring the last of the kerosene. He suddenly threw the can down. It crashed and rolled, echoing loudly against the stone floor. But when he spoke, his voice remained calm. "What's the matter, Carlyn? Feeling a little scared?"

She nodded, her gray eyes pleading.

"You're going to have to beg, you know," he said softly.

She yelled into the gag, making only a strangled cry.

"And you're going to have to do better than that," he told with a laugh. "I can't understand a word you're saying."

Carlyn watched in horror as he flicked open the first cage. The five white rats inside it backed away from Bobby. But as he moved on, opening the next cage, and the next, Carlyn could see the rats mov-

134

ing toward the open cage doors. Their whiskers trembled as they sniffed the air. Finally, one rat jumped out of its cage onto the floor. Then another.

Bobby was opening cage after cage after cage. Carlyn wriggled with all her might, dragging herself backward across the floor, away from the rats. But now he was opening cages on the other wall. She started crawling straight back.

Bobby was near the door of the lab now. He was holding a bell, one of the ones used to signal to the rats that they'd be fed. He rang the bell. "It's dinnertime," he called. "Come and get it!"

# CHAPTER 24

His eyes narrowed and his head whipped around as there was the sound of something crashing in one of the nearby labs. "Be right back," he told Carlyn. "Make sure our little friends eat well."

His laughter rang in Carlyn's ears as he disappeared out into the hallway. She kept inching backward until she couldn't go any farther. She gave a small sob of defeat as she felt her back hit the wall. Three of the largest rats began to move toward her curiously. Carlyn twisted her body violently to the left and came up against the wall again, jamming her shoulder hard.

The rats were all around her now, staring at her, moving closer. A few of them stood on their hind legs, sniffing the air. She kicked her legs violently. The rats watched her.

Then they started coming closer.

Carlyn moaned in terror as the boldest one put its paws on her bound wrist. She couldn't see it. She was lying on her side and her wrists were tied behind her. But she could feel its tiny nails digging into her skin, its tongue licking her. She jerked away from it only to find another rat crawling up onto her shoulder, making its way toward her exposed neck.

She screamed into the gag as small sharp teeth sunk deep into her ankle.

Carlyn struggled against the ropes, trying to twist, roll, flail—anything to get the rats off her. Her ankle throbbed where she'd been bit. But the rats were coming from all sides now. A large white one hovered behind her ear, sniffing delicately, and she knew that at any second she'd feel its teeth. Screaming into the gag, she kicked with all her might.

They're going to eat me, she thought in panic. They're going to eat me alive.

Something grabbed her. Her first thought was that a rat was biting her arm. But then she saw her. D.J. The girl's eyes were wide with fear as she helped Carlyn sit up and brushed the rats away. To Carlyn's amazement D.J. then reached into the book bag that hung from one shoulder and pulled out a pocket knife. Within seconds she'd cut off the gag. Next she began sawing on the thick ropes that bound Carlyn's hands and feet.

"I set up a distraction," she whispered. "I threw my calculator at one of the glass beakers next door."

"That's what that crash was?" Carlyn asked, her mouth sore from the gag.

D.J. nodded. "And we probably only have a few seconds before he figures it out and comes back in here."

"Then go and get help before it's too late!" Carlyn urged her. "Don't wait for me!"

"I'm not leaving you alone with him," D.J. said simply.

Carlyn felt the ropes fall from her wrists and began to rub them, trying to restore her circulation. The whole process was disgusting, considering she was covered with peanut butter. D.J. freed her feet next, and Carlyn stood up shakily. Following D.J., she headed for the door, picking her way over the chattering rats.

The hallway stank of kerosene. I have to get out of here, Carlyn thought frantically. She didn't know where Bobby was, but she couldn't chance his catching her again. She started to run, motioning for D.J. to follow. Behind her she heard D.J. say, "Wait!" but she was too scared to stop.

As she turned the corner D.J. caught up to her. "Where are you going?" D.J. demanded. "The stairs are that way."

Carlyn turned with a groan, knowing D.J. was right.

They started in the other direction, but they didn't get far. Bobby was coming down the hall-

138

way, heading back toward the lab. He saw them and a slow grin lit his face. "Well, well, well," he said. "The two happy lab partners. Now that's an interesting twist."

Carlyn froze, but D.J. yanked on her hand and suddenly they were racing in the opposite direction, running for their lives.

The long hallway dead-ended in a window with a lab on either side. Carlyn grabbed one of the doorknobs with two greasy hands and pulled. Locked. She tugged at the other door with no better results.

Bobby was coming toward them from the other end of the hall. He walked slowly, deliberately, each footstep bringing him closer and closer.

Carlyn suddenly realized that the lab door had a magnet strip next to the lock. She reached into her pocket for her campus ID.

"Hurry!" D.J. urged her.

Carlyn was hurrying, but her hand was jammed in the tight front pocket of her jeans. She could reach the card, but her hands were so greasy, she couldn't pull it out. Desperately, Carlyn tugged at the card again and it came flying out of her pocket, landing on the floor.

Bobby looked at her, shook his head in mock amazement, and started to laugh. But D.J. picked up the ID card and slashed at the magnetic strip.

Nothing happened.

Bobby laughed louder. "Aren't you forgetting something, Carlyn? As far as this university is concerned, you're already dead. It's okay. In a few minutes, they'll be right."

He was only ten feet away, and coming closer with each step.

For a moment, D.J. and Carlyn stared at each other, frozen in terror. Then D.J. reached into her pocket and pulled out her own ID.

Bobby dove forward. Carlyn sidestepped, but there was nowhere for D.J. to go. Bobby barreled right into her.

The horrible sound of glass shattering filled the hallway. D.J. fell backward, flailing her arms. Carlyn heard her own screams as she watched D.J. fall straight out the third-story window.

Bobby went through the glass as well, but he caught himself on the edge of the window frame. Carlyn fumbled desperately with the ID card, slapping it through the magnetic strip as she saw him pull himself over the sill and back through the shattered window. "Please open," she prayed. "Please open!"

Carlyn watched horrified as Bobby stepped back into the hallway. He was covered with glass and blood, and he was grinning that awful grin.

*Click.* The ID card worked—the lock on the door was open! Carlyn twisted the doorknob and ducked inside the deserted lab just as Bobby dove for her.

He caught her feet. Carlyn went down. Flipping over, she kicked out hard, catching her attacker in the face. Bobby let out a furious yell as they both scrambled back up.

140

Carlyn backed away wildly, careening through the dark lab. She knocked into things—a stack of petri dishes, a textbook, a chair. A glass cabinet swayed as she brushed against it, then fell with a deafening crash.

"Poor little Carlyn," Bobby said. "She's so scared she's bumping into everything."

He lunged for her. She darted around a table, trying to keep it between him and her.

It was dark in the lab, but there was some moonlight shining through the windows, and Carlyn's eyes were adjusting to the darkness. She was standing with her back to a counter lined with Bunsen burners.

She made a run for the door. But Bobby blocked her way, backing her up against the counter again. In desperation Carlyn turned and grabbed the nearest burner. Working on instinct, she turned the gas knob and fumbled for the nearest flint lighter. Bobby grabbed her hair and yanked her head straight back just as she lit the gas. But she had the advantage she needed—she managed to turn and hold the plume of ice-blue flame in front of his face.

Bobby screamed and leapt back.

Carlyn backed out of the lab, holding the burner in front of her as if it were a weapon.

"You might as well give up it now," Bobby sneered. "You know I'll just take it from you."

"Stay away from me," Carlyn ordered, her voice trembling. "If you come near me, I'll burn you, I swear it."

Bobby shook his head. "No, you won't. You're too scared." He began to hum. "Scared to death . . . scared to death . . . Little Carlyn's scared to death."

He backed her out of the darkened lab and back into the hallway. Carlyn kept the burner in front of her. Her eyes never left Bobby. He was mad, she realized. Utterly and completely insane. She'd never be able to reason with him or fight him. She'd have to find a way to outwit him. Maybe if she could just keep enough distance between them, she'd make it out of the building.

"How long do you think you can keep this up, Carlyn?" Bobby was asking. "You know I'm going to get you, just like I got Leigh and Ben. Might as well get it over with, Carlyn."

"No," she said, shaking her head.

Bobby smiled. "You'd rather drag it out? That's all right, too." And then he did something she hadn't counted on. He lunged for the Bunsen burner.

Carlyn tried to raise her arm just high enough to keep the burner away from him, but it fell from her hand and dropped to the floor, touching a spot where the floor was wet and dark.

"No!!!" Carlyn screamed, realizing at once what the flame had touched—the kerosene Bobby had spilled!

For an instant she was blinded by a bright white flash. And then the hallway burst into flames.

142

# CHAPTER 25

Carlyn stood paralyzed by terror as fire raced down the hallway. The whole floor blazed to life. A wave of heat crashed into her, followed by thick clouds of smoke.

Alarms started shrieking. Something whirred overhead and then water was blasting down, mixing with the grease all over her body.

Bobby was running away down the hallway. Carlyn turned the other way. There was—she thought she could see it through the smoke—a fire escape out this window. She shoved herself through. The glass shards that were still stuck in the window frame raked through her clothes.

D.J. was lying there on the metal platform. Carlyn bent down and shook her. "D.J.?"

There was no response. Please be alive, Carlyn prayed. "D.J.? *Dee-Jay!*"

Carlyn pulled the other girl up by her shoulders. She was definitely breathing. "D.J.," she pleaded, shaking her.

D.J. gave a soft, almost inaudible moan.

"Fire!" Carlyn shouted.

There were fire alarms going off all over the building now, a whole chorus of piercing electronic blasts, bleats, wails, and sirens. Carlyn was coughing and weeping as acrid black smoke billowed out the window, enveloping them. She had seen Bobby running the other way, but her whole body was tensed, waiting for him to burst out the window at her.

She climbed over D.J. and took a few steps down the ladder. Then she started pulling D.J. down after her. *"Hurry!"* she screamed.

D.J. was coughing and choking. But she was moving, slowly but surely climbing down.

Carlyn glanced up at the window they'd escaped from. Had Bobby escaped too? she wondered. Or was he trapped inside the building? Part of her hoped he was; part of her prayed he was dead.

D.J. took one hand off the ladder as she fell into another violent coughing fit. Carlyn pounded her on the back. "C'mon, just move!"

They kept climbing backward, downward. Above them the fire had spread across the entire third floor. Carlyn was drenched in blackened

144

sweat. Her hair and throat and skin all felt singed. "That's it," she called up at D.J. "You can make it. C'mon."

"Yeah," Bobby called up from the platform just below her. "Come on."

# CHAPTER 26

obby was standing right underneath her on the second-floor landing. His skin and clothes were blackened with smoke, and his blond hair was gone entirely. It had been a wig, Carlyn realized. His own hair, a short dark stubble, grew close to the scalp; he was almost bald. He was also drenched from the sprinklers, and covered with gooey, drying blood. And despite it all, he was grinning.

"Bobby's back," he taunted her.

Carlyn could hear D.J. weeping above her. She felt a bizarre sense of amazement as she realized that she had no more tears left, and no more fear. Everything in her life had been reduced to one simple fact: Bobby was going to kill her. That was all there was to it. This was the end.

146

Suddenly, there was a whoosh and a burst of light as the flame roared into the second-floor lab near where Bobby was standing. He turned, just for a split second.

And then came the explosion.

It blew out all the lab windows on the second floor and the fire escape landing as well.

Clutching the ladder, Carlyn closed her eyes. D.J. was screaming. So was she, she realized. She opened her eyes again. Above and below them, the fire was still raging. But Bobby was gone.

"Look!" cried D.J. She was pointing into one of the trees that lined the back of the building. Smoke was everywhere. Carlyn had no idea what D.J. was pointing at.

Then she saw, through the smoke, Bobby's bloody hand, clutching a tree branch. Slowly, slowly, the hand let go. There was a scream. Something was falling.

And an instant later there was a sickening thud as Bobby landed flat on his back on the cement below. He lay still, staring up at Carlyn. His eyes were open and blank. He was dead.

Carlyn remained paralyzed on the fire escape. There was no way down; she and D.J. remained suspended over the missing second-floor landing. But she heard sirens in the distance, and for the first time in hours she felt hope again.

Minutes later the natural sciences building was surrounded with fire trucks, ambulances, police cars. The revolving flashing lights added their garish glow to the wild orange light of the leaping flames.

Walkie-talkies blared. Everyone was shouting. Fire fighters sent a ladder up beside Carlyn and D.J. and then helped them down. On the ground paramedics led Carlyn one way, D.J. another. They wanted Carlyn to go to the hospital.

"I'm okay," she said firmly. She pulled away. She had to see this through. She had to know.

"Where are you going?" a medic yelled after her. But she pushed her way back through the chaos, headed toward the base of the building.

She was just in time to see the medics put Bobby in a body bag. They zipped up the bag. Then they loaded the bag into an ambulance.

Someone was standing next to her. She turned. It was D.J. D.J. threw her arms around her, and they hugged.

"D.J., I'm sorry about everything—" Carlyn began.

"It's okay," D.J. told her. "I figured out that the stuff that was happening wasn't your fault. Or mine."

"You saved my life," Carlyn said gratefully.

D.J. shrugged. "Well, when I came up to the lab to get my notebook and saw you all tied up, I had to do *something*."

"I can't tell you how glad I am that you did." Carlyn smiled at her ex-partner. She only had one more question. "D.J.," she said tentatively, "do you think we could give it another try? Being lab partners again, I mean."

D.J. grinned up at her. "Friends, definitely. Lab partners . . . let me think about that one."

Carlyn called Jamie collect from the nearest campus phone. "He's dead, Jamie," she said. Her voice sounded so calm, so strangely calm. "It's over. He's gone forever. And he'll never bother us again."

There was silence on the other end as Carlyn told Jamie the whole story. Then she heard Jamie start to cry. "Oh my God," she murmured. "They got him. They really got him. Bobby Wimmer is dead."

"I better go now," Carlyn said. "I'll call you later, okay?"

"Okay," Jamie sobbed. "Thank God you're all right!"

After she hung up, Carlyn started toward her dorm. Then she turned around and headed back toward the science building. She stood for a long time, watching the huge building burn. Somehow, she couldn't look away. It was as if she needed to see this through to the end. She reached up when she felt something wet on her cheek, and realized she was crying. It was sinking in. What she had told Jamie was really true. It was over—over at last.

# EPILOGUE

Lester Conklin, head of the county morgue, had rarely seen so much action in a single night. First they brought in the car crash victims—three teenagers out driving drunk had smashed head-on into a tree. Smart move. Next they brought in an old man who'd had a heart attack, then some psycho college kid from the campus who had tried to burn down the science building or something.

The body bags were lying on tables all over the room, waiting to be logged in and tagged. Let them wait. They weren't going anywhere.

But neither was he. Sighing, he went out to the front office to call his wife and tell her not to wait up.

* * *

As Conklin left the room a bloody finger poked up from the top of one of the body bags, pushing at the zipper. Then another finger emerged. Then the whole bloody hand.

The hand pushed the zipper down slowly. Bobby climbed out as quickly and quietly as he could.

They thought he had died. Good. The careless work of those paramedics would come in very handy. He had a lot of work left to do. He didn't need anyone worrying about him. As far as they were concerned, he no longer existed.

Listening for the sound of Conklin's return, he picked up a clipboard on the desk. It was labeled "Night Log." And there were the body tags.

Already new plans were forming in his head. He'd switch the tags. They'd bury someone else in his place. Perfect.

Yes.

They hadn't seen the last of Bobby Wimmer.

He'd be back.

# Scared yet?
# Watch out for
## SCARED TO DEATH 3:
# BRIDESMAIDS IN BLACK

Bobby is furious.

When his girlfriend Debbie finds out about his plan to kill the Five, she tries to stop him. Big mistake. Nothing will stop him. Nothing must stand in his way.

The Five are to blame for everything that's gone wrong in his life. And now they're going to pay.

He's going to get them—the three that are left: Watch out, Carlyn. Watch out, Brooke. Watch out, Jamie.

All three are going back to Middletown to be bridesmaids at their friend Danielle's wedding.

Bobby isn't invited, but he'll be there.

To see three pretty bridesmaids, all dressed in black.

It's Danielle's wedding—but it's Carlyn, Brooke, and Jamie's funeral.

# A SELECTION OF TITLES
# AVAILABLE FROM BANTAM BOOKS

THE PRICES SHOWN BELOW WERE CORRECT AT THE TIME OF
GOING TO PRESS. HOWEVER TRANSWORLD PUBLISHERS
RESERVE THE RIGHT TO SHOW NEW RETAIL PRICES ON
COVERS WHICH MAY DIFFER FROM THOSE PREVIOUSLY
ADVERTISED IN THE TEXT OR ELSEWHERE.

All Bantam Books are available at your bookshop or newsagent, or can be ordered
from the following address:

Transworld Publishers Ltd,
Cash Sales Department,
P.O. Box 11, Falmouth, Cornwall TR10 9EN

Please send a cheque or postal order (no currency) and allow £1.00 for postage and
packing for one book, an additional 50p for a second book, and an additional 30p for
each subsequent book ordered to a maximum charge of £3.00 if ordering seven books
or more.

Overseas customers, including Eire, please allow £2.00 for postage and packing for
the first book, an additional £1.00 for a second book, and an additional 50p for each
subsequent title ordered.

NAME (Block Letters) ........................................................................................................

ADDRESS ........................................................................................................

........................................................................................................